THE FOLGER LIBRARY SHAKESPEARE

Designed to make Shakespeare's classic plays available to the general reader, each edition contains a reliable text with modernized spelling and punctuation, scene-by-scene plot summaries, and explanatory notes clarifying obscure and obsolete expressions. An interpretive essay and accounts of Shakespeare's life and theater form an instructive preface to each play.

Louis B. Wright, General Editor, was the Director of the Folger Shakespeare Library from 1948 until his retirement in 1968. He is the author of *Middle-Class Culture in Elizabethan England, Religion and Empire, Shakespeare for Everyman,* and many other books and essays on the history and literature of the Tudor and Stuart periods.

Virginia Lamar, Assistant Editor, served as research assistant to the Director and Executive Secretary of the Folger Shakespeare Library from 1946 until her death in 1968. She is the author of *English Dress in the Age of Shakespeare* and *Travel and Roads in England,* and coeditor of William Strachey's *Historie of Travell into Virginia Britania.*

The Folger Library General Reader's Shakespeare

THE
MERRY WIVES
OF
WINDSOR

by

WILLIAM
SHAKESPEARE

WASHINGTON SQUARE PRESS
PUBLISHED BY POCKET BOOKS

New York   London   Toronto   Sydney   Tokyo   Singapore

A Washington Square Press Publication of
POCKET BOOKS, a division of Simon & Schuster Inc.
1230 Avenue of the Americas, New York, NY 10020

Copyright © 1964 by Simon & Schuster Inc.

ISBN: 0-671-73143-2

First Pocket Books printing February 1965

15   14   13   12   11   10   9   8   7

WASHINGTON SQUARE PRESS and WSP colophon are
registered trademarks of Simon & Schuster Inc.

Printed in the U.S.A.

Preface

This edition of *The Merry Wives of Windsor* is designed to make available a readable text of one of Shakespeare's funniest comedies. In the centuries since Shakespeare, many changes have occurred in the meanings of words, and some clarification of Shakespeare's vocabulary may be helpful. To provide the reader with necessary notes in the most accessible format, we have placed them on the pages facing the text that they explain. We have tried to make these notes as brief and simple as possible. Preliminary to the text we have also included a brief statement of essential information about Shakespeare and his stage. Readers desiring more detailed information should refer to the books suggested in the references, and if still further information is needed, the bibliographies in those books will provide the necessary clues to the literature of the subject.

The early texts of Shakespeare's plays provide only scattered stage directions and no indications of setting, and it is conventional for modern editors to add these to clarify the action. Such additions, and additions to entrances and exits, as well as many indications of act and scene division, are placed in square brackets.

All illustrations are from material in the Folger Library collections.

L. B. W.
V. A. L.

April 28, 1964

Theatrically Effective Comedy

Victorian critics found the Falstaff of *The Merry Wives of Windsor* too gross for their tastes and condemned Shakespeare for writing a play lacking in those genteel qualities that literary men of the nineteenth century thought Shakespeare ought to have displayed. Forgetting that Shakespeare was a practical man of the theatre, ready to capitalize upon the popularity of a character who had already won the plaudits of Elizabethan audiences, even later scholar-critics have worried about the "degeneration" in Shakespeare's concept of the fat knight and the "claptrap" introduced in *The Merry Wives of Windsor*.

The truth is that this play is highly effective upon the stage and has enjoyed a more continuous life in the playhouse than most of Shakespeare's comedies. It was written to be seen on the stage rather than to be read in the study, although its dialogue is funnier in reading than that of many plays more esteemed by critics. Shakespeare the successful producer knew precisely what he was about when he put together *The Merry Wives of Windsor*, and we too can share the enjoyment experienced by the

Elizabethan audience if we disregard "literary" criticism that misses the point of Shakespearean farce.

The epilogue of *Henry IV, Part 2* promised that if the public was "not too much cloyed with fat meat, our humble author will continue the story, with Sir John in it, and make you merry with fair Katherine of France. Where, for any thing I know, Falstaff shall die of a sweat, unless already 'a be killed with your hard opinions." But in *Henry V* Shakespeare did not carry out his promise, and Falstaff died off stage. The Falstaff scenes in the two parts of *Henry IV* remained so popular that Shakespeare may have regretted the necessity of dispensing with Falstaff in *Henry V*. Demand for more comic scenes with the roguish knight may have induced him to write one more play utilizing this character.

Early in the eighteenth century a story gained currency that Queen Elizabeth herself commanded Shakespeare to write a play showing Falstaff in love. John Dennis, who made an adaptation of *The Merry Wives of Windsor* in 1702, was the first to publish this tale; he declared that the Queen was so eager to see it acted "that she commanded it to be finished in fourteen days." Nicholas Rowe in 1709 repeated the story, either taking it from Dennis or from their common source.

This explanation of the composition of *The Merry Wives of Windsor* cannot be proved, but it is easy to believe. From what we know about Queen Elizabeth, she had a robust sense of humor capable of

appreciating Falstaff, and it is not out of character
for her to order the dramatist to show Falstaff in
love. This is the most English of Shakespeare's
comedies, and the Queen herself was proud to de-
clare herself "mere English." And it is not out of
character for Shakespeare to supply scenes of
boisterous comedy portraying the lecherous old
braggart discomfited by the two virtuous wives of
Windsor, who themselves loved a practical joke.

No profound lessons are implicit in this play, and
no refinements of aesthetic theory can be found by
the most diligent searcher. Shakespeare was no
white-livered aesthete himself, and he clearly enjoyed the contemplation of the predicaments that
he created for Falstaff. These facts of Elizabethan
life have been too often disregarded by the writers
of commentaries on Shakespeare. If Queen Elizabeth was so coarse as to want to see Falstaff in love,
said Hartley Coleridge, she was "a gross-minded old
baggage." And Edward Dowden asserted that the
Falstaff of *The Merry Wives of Windsor* was not the
wit from *Henry IV* but "a fat rogue, brought forward from the back premises of the poet's imagination in Falstaff's clothes."

After surveying this type of criticism of *The
Merry Wives of Windsor*, Sir Edmund Chambers,
ever one of the most sensible commentators on
Shakespeare, observes that we ought not consider
this play a "literary crime" (as one critic described
it) for "Shakespeare was not only a poet and analyst
but also, and primarily, a practical playwright" who

Queen Elizabeth at Windsor for an investiture of Knights of the Garter.
From Elias Ashmole, *The Institution, Laws, and Ceremonies of the Most Noble Order of the Garter* (1672).

himself would have greeted the worry of the aesthetes about Falstaff's degeneration with a roar of gusty laughter.

Although *The Merry Wives of Windsor* shows evidence of hasty writing, it is much better constructed than some of Shakespeare's other plays (*Henry IV*, for example). It moves rapidly, its dialogue is racy, its humor is earthy but healthy, and its farcical action provides laughter and entertainment for all but the most tender-minded of readers or spectators.

Internal evidence in the play suggests that it may have been written for performance at a feast of the Knights of the Garter, with the Queen present. Professor Leslie Hotson in *Shakespeare versus Shallow* suggested that it had been written hurriedly for a celebration in connection with an installation of Knights of the Garter in 1597. The patron of Shakespeare's own acting company, Lord Hunsdon, the Lord Chamberlain, was created a Knight of the Garter at that time. A passage referring to "Our radiant Queen" and a long simile descriptive of insignia of the Garter Knights in Act V, Sc. v, would have little point unless the play was written for some ceremony of the order. The setting at Windsor and frequent allusions to the locale and to familiar scenes in the deer park and surrounding terrain would have been relevant to the fact that the home of the Garter order was St. George's Chapel in Windsor Castle, where investitures took place. Doubtless many topical allusions, hidden in the dialogue, were obvious to the spectators but are now lost to us.

The discomfiture of an importunate old suitor by two sprightly women was a theme that would have been congenial to the Virgin Queen. Shakespeare himself delighted in portraying women who had the wit and ingenuity to circumvent men, and if Mistress Ford and Mistress Page are not the equals of the women in Shakespeare's romantic comedies, nevertheless they give the illusion of reality. If the Queen wanted to see Falstaff in comic entanglements resulting from his amorous pursuits, Shakespeare provided incidents in full measure to please Her Majesty and her court. Partisans of the Falstaff of *Henry IV* have objected that no longer does Shakespeare endow the fat knight with the nimble wit that enabled him in the earlier plays to extricate himself from every embarrassing situation. On the contrary, in *The Merry Wives of Windsor* he is easily duped, even with the most transparent devices. But wiser men than Falstaff have been the dupes of women, and Shakespeare was at least doing no violence to dramatic tradition in making the vain old braggart soldier the victim of his own amorous stratagems.

DATE, HISTORY, AND TEXT

No explicit source for *The Merry Wives of Windsor* is known. A common motif in Italian stories and in comedies of intrigue is the lover hidden in a barrel, basket, or closet. Other situations in the play are not uncommon. The story of Herne the Hunter probably comes from local folklore; many years after the play, an oak called Herne's Oak was pointed out in Windsor Park. Because of its alleged Shakespearean interest, a dealer sold Henry Clay Folger a worm-eaten walking stick said to have been cut from "Herne's Oak." In the later eighteenth century, Windsor discovered two houses that it assigned to Page and Ford. No curio dealer has yet come forward with Falstaff's buck basket.

As Chambers points out, the essential plot in *The Merry Wives*—a would-be lover outwitted and tricked by his intended conquest—is an ancient literary convention exemplified in many French fabliaux, in English literature in Chaucer's "Miller's Tale," and later on the stage in the plots of a number of popular comedies. Shakespeare in *The Merry Wives* utilized a conventional situation, but he gave it a fresh interest by vivid localization and deft touches of characterization. All in all, conventional farce though it is, *The Merry Wives* transcends its type and has sufficient intrinsic merit as comedy to keep it alive through the ages.

Certain elements in the play have persuaded some scholars that Shakespeare may have reworked an earlier play in his haste to produce *The Merry Wives* and that fragments of the prototype remain imbedded in the text. A play called *The Jealous Comedy*, produced by Philip Henslowe in 1593, may have furnished Shakespeare with his plot, they suggest. *The Merry Wives of Windsor* as we have it today does betray careless and imperfect revision of some sort, but whether this indicates a reworking of *The Jealous Comedy* may be doubted.

Some incidents have little relation to anything else in the play. For example, the allusion to horse-stealing by three Germans, apparently attached to a German duke, is completely extraneous and appears to reflect popular interest in Count Mömpelgart, later the Duke of Württemberg, who visited England in 1592 and henceforth besought Queen Elizabeth to make him a Knight of the Garter, an honor that he finally was granted in 1597, although his formal investiture did not occur until the first year of King James's reign. If the play was produced in connection with Garter rites in 1597, references to the German nobleman would have been more topical than they otherwise seem. Mömpelgart and his followers were disliked and made themselves somewhat ridiculous; hence a hit at visiting Germans would have been appreciated. In the 1602 Quarto version of *The Merry Wives* (IV, v) occurs a phrase "cozen garmombles" which in the Folio text was changed to "Cozen-Iermans" (cousin-germans). Queen Elizabeth called the Count "our Cousin Mumpellgart." "Garmombles" (which means "confusion") is obviously a comic twisting of the Count's name. The fact that this subplot is not developed and the reader never learns the full story of the horse-stealing may reflect revision of the play for performance at a later date when Mömpelgart's visit and his election as a Knight of the Garter would no longer have been

topical. Other evidences of revision in the play indi-
cate haste or carelessness, or both, on the part of the
author.

The first printing of *The Merry Wives of Windsor*
was the very corrupt Quarto brought out in 1602.
The title page stated that it had seen divers performances both before Her Majesty and elsewhere.
Despite the plausibility of 1597 as the date of first
performance, several scholars believe that it was
first performed in 1600 or early 1601. The Quarto
seems to have been reconstructed from memory,
perhaps by the actor who played the part of the
host. A Second Quarto appeared in 1619, an un-
corrected reprint of the First Quarto with minor
changes. The first authentic printing of the play was
that in the First Folio of 1623, which is a relatively
good text. The present editors, like all others, have
used the Folio as the basis of their edition. Suggestions for improvements of a few readings, either
confused or corrupt in the Folio, are found in the
First Quarto, which also provides a few stage directions not in the Folio text.

The Merry Wives of Windsor has had a long and
honorable stage history. It was revived at Court in
1604 and 1638. After the theatres reopened at the
Restoration in 1660, this play was one of Shakespeare's revived at the Theatre Royal and it continued to be acted at intervals. John Dennis' adaptation, *The Comical Gallant, or, The Amours of Sir
John Falstaff,* was performed briefly at Drury Lane
in 1702 but proved less acceptable than Shake-

speare's original, which a few years later was again
revived on the stage of Lincoln's Inn Fields. James
Quin, one of the most famous actors of the first half
of the eighteenth century, made Falstaff in *The
Merry Wives* one of his best roles. David Garrick, as
manager of Drury Lane, included the play among
those frequently revived. It remained popular on
both sides of the Atlantic throughout most of the
nineteenth century and has been often seen during
the twentieth century. Indeed, *The Merry Wives of
Windsor* has been one of the most frequently acted
of Shakespeare's comedies and has generally met
with approval and applause.

THE AUTHOR

As early as 1598 Shakespeare was so well known as
a literary and dramatic craftsman that Francis
Meres, in his *Palladis Tamia: Wits Treasury*, referred in flattering terms to him as "mellifluous and
honey-tongued Shakespeare," famous for his *Venus
and Adonis*, his *Lucrece*, and "his sugared sonnets,"
which were circulating "among his private friends."
Meres observes further that "as Plautus and Seneca
are accounted the best for comedy and tragedy
among the Latins, so Shakespeare among the English is the most excellent in both kinds for the
stage," and he mentions a dozen plays that had
made a name for Shakespeare. He concludes with
the remark that "the Muses would speak with

Shakespeare's fine filed phrase if they would speak English."

To those acquainted with the history of the Elizabethan and Jacobean periods, it is incredible that anyone should be so naïve or ignorant as to doubt the reality of Shakespeare as the author of the plays that bear his name. Yet so much nonsense has been written about other "candidates" for the plays that it is well to remind readers that no credible evidence that would stand up in a court of law has ever been adduced to prove either that Shakespeare did not write his plays or that anyone else wrote them. All the theories offered for the authorship of Francis Bacon, the Earl of Derby, the Earl of Oxford, the Earl of Hertford, Christopher Marlowe, and a score of other candidates are mere conjectures spun from the active imaginations of persons who confuse hypothesis and conjecture with evidence.

As Meres's statement of 1598 indicates, Shakespeare was already a popular playwright whose name carried weight at the box office. The obvious reputation of Shakespeare as early as 1598 makes the effort to prove him a myth one of the most absurd in the history of human perversity.

The anti-Shakespeareans talk darkly about a plot of vested interests to maintain the authorship of Shakespeare. Nobody has any vested interest in Shakespeare, but every scholar is interested in the truth and in the quality of evidence advanced by special pleaders who set forth hypotheses in place of facts.

The anti-Shakespeareans base their arguments upon a few simple premises, all of them false. These false premises are that Shakespeare was an unlettered yokel without any schooling, that nothing is known about Shakespeare, and that only a noble lord or the equivalent in background could have written the plays. The facts are that more is known about Shakespeare than about most dramatists of his day, that he had a very good education, acquired in the Stratford Grammar School, that the plays show no evidence of profound book learning, and that the knowledge of kings and courts evident in the plays is no greater than any intelligent young man could have picked up at second hand. Most anti-Shakespeareans are naïve and betray an obvious snobbery. The author of their favorite plays, they imply, must have had a college diploma framed and hung on his study wall like the one in their dentist's office, and obviously so great a writer must have had a title or some equally significant evidence of exalted social background. They forget that genius has a way of cropping up in unexpected places and that none of the great creative writers of the world got his inspiration in a college or university course.

William Shakespeare was the son of John Shakespeare of Stratford-upon-Avon, a substantial citizen of that small but busy market town in the center of the rich agricultural county of Warwick. John

Shakespeare kept a shop, what we would call a general store; he dealt in wool and other produce and gradually acquired property. As a youth, John Shakespeare had learned the trade of glover and leather worker. There is no contemporary evidence that the elder Shakespeare was a butcher, though the anti-Shakespeareans like to talk about the ignorant "butcher's boy of Stratford." Their only evidence is a statement by gossipy John Aubrey, more than a century after William Shakespeare's birth, that young William followed his father's trade, and when he killed a calf, "he would do it in a high style and make a speech." We would like to believe the story true, but Aubrey is not a very credible witness.

John Shakespeare probably continued to operate a farm at Snitterfield that his father had leased. He married Mary Arden, daughter of his father's landlord, a man of some property. The third of their eight children was William, baptized on April 26, 1564, and probably born three days before. At least, it is conventional to celebrate April 23 as his birthday.

The Stratford records give considerable information about John Shakespeare. We know that he held several municipal offices including those of alderman and mayor. In 1580 he was in some sort of legal difficulty and was fined for neglecting a summons of the Court of Queen's Bench requiring him to appear at Westminster and be bound over to keep the peace.

As a citizen and alderman of Stratford, John Shakespeare was entitled to send his son to the grammar school free. Though the records are lost, there can be no reason to doubt that this is where young William received his education. As any student of the period knows, the grammar schools provided the basic education in Latin learning and literature. The Elizabethan grammar school is not to be confused with modern grammar schools. Many cultivated men of the day received all their formal education in the grammar schools. At the universities in this period a student would have received little training that would have inspired him to be a creative writer. At Stratford young Shakespeare would have acquired a familiarity with Latin and some little knowledge of Greek. He would have read Latin authors and become acquainted with the plays of Plautus and Terence. Undoubtedly, in this period of his life he received that stimulation to read and explore for himself the world of ancient and modern history which he later utilized in his plays. The youngster who does not acquire this type of intellectual curiosity *before* college days rarely develops as a result of a college course the kind of mind Shakespeare demonstrated. His learning in books was anything but profound, but he clearly had the probing curiosity that sent him in search of information, and he had a keenness in the observation of nature and of humankind that finds reflection in his poetry.

There is little documentation for Shakespeare's

boyhood. There is little reason why there should be. Nobody knew that he was going to be a dramatist about whom any scrap of information would be prized in the centuries to come. He was merely an active and vigorous youth of Stratford, perhaps assisting his father in his business, and no Boswell bothered to write down facts about him. The most important record that we have is a marriage license issued by the Bishop of Worcester on November 27, 1582, to permit William Shakespeare to marry Anne Hathaway, seven or eight years his senior; furthermore, the Bishop permitted the marriage after reading the banns only once instead of three times, evidence of the desire for haste. The need was explained on May 26, 1583, when the christening of Susanna, daughter of William and Anne Shakespeare, was recorded at Stratford. Two years later, on February 2, 1585, the records show the birth of twins to the Shakespeares, a boy and a girl who were christened Hamnet and Judith.

What William Shakespeare was doing in Stratford during the early years of his married life, or when he went to London, we do not know. It has been conjectured that he tried his hand at schoolteaching, but that is a mere guess. There is a legend that he left Stratford to escape a charge of poaching in the park of Sir Thomas Lucy of Charlecote, but there is no proof of this. There is also a legend that when first he came to London he earned his living by holding horses outside a playhouse and presently was given employment inside, but there is nothing better than eighteenth-century hearsay for this. How Shakespeare broke into the London theatres as a dramatist and actor we do not know. But lack of information is not surprising, for Elizabethans did not write their autobiographies, and we know even less about the lives of many writers and some men of affairs than we know about Shakespeare. By 1592 he was so well established and popular that he incurred the envy of the dramatist and pamphleteer Robert Greene, who referred to him as an "upstart crow . . . in his own conceit the only Shake-scene in a country." From this time onward, contemporary allusions and references in legal documents enable the scholar to chart Shakespeare's career with greater accuracy than is possible with most other Elizabethan dramatists.

By 1594 Shakespeare was a member of the company of actors known as the Lord Chamberlain's Men. After the accession of James I, in 1603, the company would have the sovereign for their patron and would be known as the King's Men. During the period of its greatest prosperity, this company would have as its principal theatres the Globe and the Blackfriars. Shakespeare was both an actor and a shareholder in the company. Tradition has assigned him such acting roles as Adam in *As You Like It* and the Ghost in *Hamlet*, a modest place on the stage that suggests that he may have had other duties in the management of the company. Such conclusions, however, are based on surmise.

What we do know is that his plays were popular and that he was highly successful in his vocation. His first play may have been *The Comedy of Errors*, acted perhaps in 1591. Certainly this was one of his earliest plays. The three parts of *Henry VI* were acted sometime between 1590 and 1592. Critics are not in agreement about precisely how much Shakespeare wrote of these three plays. *Richard III* probably dates from 1593. With this play Shakespeare captured the imagination of Elizabethan audiences, then enormously interested in historical plays. With *Richard III* Shakespeare also gave an interpretation pleasing to the Tudors of the rise to power of the grandfather of Queen Elizabeth. From this time onward, Shakespeare's plays followed on the stage in rapid succession: *Titus Andronicus, The Taming of the Shrew, The Two Gentlemen of Verona, Love's Labor's Lost, Romeo and Juliet, Richard II, A Midsummer Night's Dream, King John, The Merchant of Venice, Henry IV (Parts 1 and 2), Much Ado about Nothing, Henry V, Julius Cæsar, As You Like It, Twelfth Night, Hamlet, The Merry Wives of Windsor, All's Well That Ends Well, Measure for Measure, Othello, King Lear,* and nine others that followed before Shakespeare retired completely, about 1613.

In the course of his career in London, he made enough money to enable him to retire to Stratford with a competence. His purchase on May 4, 1597, of New Place, then the second-largest dwelling in Stratford, a " pretty house of brick and timber," with a handsome garden, indicates his increasing prosperity. There his wife and children lived while he busied himself in the London theatres. The summer before he acquired New Place, his life was darkened by the death of his only son, Hamnet, a child of eleven. In May, 1602, Shakespeare purchased one hundred and seven acres of fertile farmland near Stratford and a few months later bought a cottage and garden across the alley from New Place. About 1611, he seems to have returned permanently to Stratford, for the next year a legal document refers to him as "William Shakespeare of Stratford-upon-Avon . . . gentleman." To achieve the desired appellation of gentleman, William Shakespeare had seen to it that the College of Heralds in 1596 granted his father a coat of arms. In one step he thus became a second-generation gentleman.

Shakespeare's daughter Susanna made a good match in 1607 with Dr. John Hall, a prominent and prosperous Stratford physician. His second daughter, Judith, did not marry until she was thirty-two years old, and then, under somewhat scandalous circumstances, she married Thomas Quiney, a Stratford vintner. On March 25, 1616, Shakespeare made his will, bequeathing his landed property to Susanna, £300 to Judith, certain sums to other relatives, and his second-best bed to his wife, Anne. Much has been made of the second-best bed, but the legacy probably indicates only that Anne liked that particular bed. Shakespeare, following the practice of the time, may have already arranged with Susanna for his wife's care. Finally, on April 23, 1616, the anniversary of his birth, William Shakespeare died, and he was buried on April 25 within the chancel of Trinity Church, as befitted an honored citizen. On August 6, 1623, a few months before the publication of the collected edition of Shakespeare's plays, Anne Shakespeare joined her husband in death.

THE PUBLICATION OF HIS PLAYS

During his lifetime Shakespeare made no effort to publish any of his plays, though eighteen appeared in print in single-play editions known as quartos. Some of these are corrupt versions known as "bad quartos." No quarto, so far as is known, had the author's approval. Plays were not considered "literature" any more than most radio and television scripts today are considered literature. Dramatists sold their plays outright to the theatrical companies and it was usually considered in the company's interest to keep plays from getting into print. To achieve a reputation as a man of letters, Shakespeare wrote his *Sonnets* and his narrative poems, *Venus and Adonis* and *The Rape of Lucrece,* but he probably never dreamed that his plays would establish his reputation as a literary genius. Only Ben Jonson, a man known for his colossal conceit, had the crust to call his plays *Works,* as he did when he published an edition in 1616. But men laughed at Ben Jonson.

After Shakespeare's death, two of his old colleagues in the King's Men, John Heminges and Henry Condell, decided that it would be a good thing to print, in more accurate versions than were then available, the plays already published and eighteen additional plays not previously published in quarto. In 1623 appeared *Mr. William Shakespeares Comedies, Histories, & Tragedies. Published according to the True Originall Copies. London. Printed by Isaac Iaggard and Ed. Blount*. This was the famous First Folio, a work that had the authority of Shakespeare's associates. The only play commonly attributed to Shakespeare that was omitted in the First Folio was *Pericles*. In their preface, "To the great Variety of Readers," Heminges and Condell state that whereas "you were abused with diverse stolen and surreptitious copies, maimed and deformed by the frauds and stealths of injurious impostors that exposed them, even those are now offered to your view cured and perfect of their limbs; and all the rest, absolute in their numbers, as he conceived them." What they used for printer's copy is one of the vexed problems of scholarship, and skilled bibliographers have devoted years of study to the question of the relation of the "copy" for the First Folio to Shakespeare's manuscripts. In some cases it is clear that the editors corrected printed quarto versions of the plays, probably by comparison with playhouse scripts. Whether these scripts were in Shakespeare's autograph is anybody's guess. No manuscript of any play in Shakespeare's handwriting has survived. Indeed, very few play manuscripts from this period by any author are extant. The Tudor and Stuart periods had not yet learned to prize autographs and authors' original manuscripts.

Since the First Folio contains eighteen plays not previously printed, it is the only source for these. For the other eighteen, which had appeared in quarto versions, the First Folio also has the authority of an edition prepared and overseen by Shakespeare's colleagues and professional associates. But since editorial standards in 1623 were far from strict, and Heminges and Condell were actors rather than editors by profession, the texts are sometimes careless. The printing and proofreading of the First Folio also left much to be desired, and some garbled passages have had to be corrected and emended. The "good quarto" texts have to be taken into account in preparing a modern edition.

Because of the great popularity of Shakespeare through the centuries, the First Folio has become a prized book, but it is not a very rare one, for it is estimated that 238 copies are extant. The Folger Shakespeare Library in Washington, D.C., has seventy-nine copies of the First Folio, collected by the founder, Henry Clay Folger, who believed that a collation of as many texts as possible would reveal significant facts about the text of Shakespeare's plays. Dr. Charlton Hinman, using an ingenious machine of his own invention for mechanical collating, has made many discoveries that throw light on Shakespeare's text and on printing practices of the day.

The probability is that the First Folio of 1623 had an edition of between 1,000 and 1,250 copies. It is believed that it sold for £1, which made it an expensive book, for £1 in 1623 was equivalent to something between $40 and $50 in modern purchasing power.

During the seventeenth century, Shakespeare was sufficiently popular to warrant three later editions in folio size, the Second Folio of 1632, the Third Folio of 1663–1664, and the Fourth Folio of 1685. The Third Folio added six other plays ascribed to Shakespeare, but these are apocryphal.

THE SHAKESPEAREAN THEATRE

The theatres in which Shakespeare's plays were performed were vastly different from those we know today. The stage was a platform that jutted out into the area now occupied by the first rows of seats on the main floor, what is called the "orchestra" in America and the "pit" in England. This platform had no curtain to come down at the ends of acts and scenes. And although simple stage properties were available, the Elizabethan theatre lacked both the machinery and the elaborate movable scenery of the modern theatre. In the rear of the platform stage was a curtained area that could be used as an inner room, a tomb, or any such scene that might be required. A balcony above this inner room, and perhaps balconies on the sides of the stage, could represent the upper deck of a ship, the entry to Juliet's room, or a prison window. A trap door in the stage provided an entrance for ghosts and devils from the nether regions, and a similar trap in the canopied structure over the stage, known as the "heavens," made it possible to let down angels on a rope. These primitive stage arrangements help to account for many elements in Elizabethan plays. For example, since there was no curtain, the dramatist frequently felt the necessity of writing into his play action to clear the stage at the ends of acts and scenes. The funeral march at the end of *Hamlet* is not there merely for atmosphere; Shakespeare had to get the corpses off the stage. The lack of scenery also freed the dramatist from undue concern about the exact location of his sets, and the physical relation of his various settings to each other did not have to be worked out with the same precision as in the modern theatre.

Before London had buildings designed exclusively for theatrical entertainment, plays were given in inns and taverns. The characteristic inn of the period had an inner courtyard with rooms opening onto balconies overlooking the yard. Players could set up their temporary stages at one end of the yard and audiences could find seats on the balconies out of the weather. The poorer sort could stand or sit on the cobblestones in the yard, which was open to the sky. The first theatres followed this construction, and throughout the Elizabethan period the large public theatres had a yard in front of the stage open to the weather, with two or three tiers of covered balconies extending around the theatre. This physical structure again influenced the writing of plays. Because a dramatist wanted the actors to be heard, he frequently wrote into his play orations that could be delivered with declamatory effect. He also provided spectacle, buffoonery, and broad jests to keep the riotous groundlings in the yard entertained and quiet.

In another respect the Elizabethan theatre differed greatly from ours. It had no actresses. All women's roles were taken by boys, sometimes recruited from the boys' choirs of the London churches. Some of these youths acted their roles with great skill and the Elizabethans did not seem to be aware of any incongruity. The first actresses on the professional English stage appeared after the Restoration of Charles II, in 1660, when exiled Englishmen brought back from France practices of the French stage.

London in the Elizabethan period, as now, was the center of theatrical interest, though wandering actors from time to time traveled through the country performing in inns, halls, and the houses of the nobility. The first professional playhouse, called simply The Theatre, was erected by James Burbage, father of Shakespeare's colleague Richard Burbage, in 1576 on lands of the old Holywell

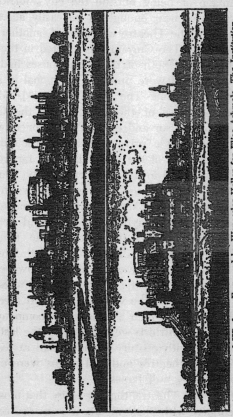

A prospect of Windsor. Engraved by Wenceslas Hollar for Elias Ashmole, *The Institution, Laws, and Ceremonies of the Most Noble Order of the Garter* (1672).

Priory adjacent to Finsbury Fields, a playground and park area just north of the city walls. It had the advantage of being outside the city's jurisdiction and yet was near enough to be easily accessible. Soon after The Theatre was opened, another playhouse called The Curtain was erected in the same neighborhood. Both of these playhouses had open courtyards and were probably polygonal in shape.

About the time The Curtain opened, Richard Farrant, Master of the Children of the Chapel Royal at Windsor and of St. Paul's, conceived the idea of opening a "private" theatre in the old monastery buildings of the Blackfriars, not far from St. Paul's Cathedral in the heart of the city. This theatre was ostensibly to train the choirboys in plays for presentation at Court, but Farrant managed to present plays to paying audiences and achieved considerable success until aristocratic neighbors complained and had the theatre closed. This first Blackfriars Theatre was significant, however, because it popularized the boy actors in a professional way and it paved the way for a second theatre in the Blackfriars, which Shakespeare's company took over more than thirty years later. By the last years of the sixteenth century, London had at least six professional theatres and still others were erected during the reign of James I.

The Globe Theatre, the playhouse that most people connect with Shakespeare, was erected early in 1599 on the Bankside, the area across the Thames from the city. Its construction had a dramatic beginning, for on the night of December 28, 1598, James Burbage's sons, Cuthbert and Richard, gathered together a crew who tore down the old theatre in Holywell and carted the timbers across the river to a site that they had chosen for a new playhouse. The reason for this clandestine operation was a row with the landowner over the lease to the Holywell property. The site chosen for the Globe was another playground outside of the city's jurisdiction, a region of somewhat unsavory character. Not far away was the Bear Garden, an amphitheatre devoted to the baiting of bears and bulls. This was also the region occupied by many houses of ill fame licensed by the Bishop of Winchester and the source of substantial revenue to him. But it was easily accessible either from London Bridge or by means of the cheap boats operated by the London watermen, and it had the great advantage of being beyond the authority of the Puritanical aldermen of London, who frowned on plays because they lured apprentices from work, filled their heads with improper ideas, and generally exerted a bad influence. The aldermen also complained that the crowds drawn together in the theatre helped to spread the plague.

The Globe was the handsomest theatre up to its time. It was a large building, apparently octagonal in shape, and open like its predecessors to the sky in the center, but capable of seating a large audience in its covered balconies. To erect and operate the Globe, the Burbages organized a syndicate composed of the leading members of the dramatic company, of which Shakespeare was a member. Since it was open to the weather and depended on natural light, plays had to be given in the afternoon. This caused no hardship in the long afternoons of an English summer, but in the winter the weather was a great handicap and discouraged all except the hardiest. For that reason, in 1608 Shakespeare's company was glad to take over the lease of the second Blackfriars Theatre, a substantial, roomy hall reconstructed within the framework of the old monastery building. This theatre was protected from the weather and its stage was artificially lighted by chandeliers of candles. This became the winter playhouse for Shakespeare's company and at once proved so popular that the congestion of traffic created an embarrassing problem. Stringent regulations had to be made for the movement of coaches in the vicinity. Shakespeare's company continued to use the Globe during the summer months. In 1613 a squib fired from a cannon during a performance of *Henry VIII* fell on the thatched roof and the Globe burned to the ground. The next year it was rebuilt.

London had other famous theatres. The Rose, just west of the Globe, was built by Philip Henslowe, a semiliterate denizen of the Bankside, who became one of the most important theatrical owners and producers of the Tudor and Stuart periods. What is more important for historians, he kept a detailed account book, which provides much of our information about theatrical history in his time. Another famous theatre on the Bankside was the Swan, which a Dutch priest, Johannes de Witt, visited in 1596. The crude drawing of the stage which he made was copied by his friend Arend van Buchell; it is one of the important pieces of contemporary evidence for theatrical construction. Among the other theatres, the Fortune, north of the city, on Golding Lane, and the Red Bull, even farther away from the city, off St. John's Street, were the most popular. The Red Bull, much frequented by apprentices, favored sensational and sometimes rowdy plays.

The actors who kept all of these theatres going were organized into companies under the protection of some noble patron. Traditionally actors had enjoyed a low reputation. In some of the ordinances they were classed as vagrants; in the phraseology of the time, "rogues, vagabonds, sturdy beggars, and common players" were all listed together as undesirables. To escape penalties often meted out to these characters, organized groups of actors managed to gain the protection of various personages of high degree. In the later years of Elizabeth's reign, a group flourished under the name of the Queen's Men; another group had the protection of the Lord Admiral and were known as the Lord Admiral's Men. Edward Alleyn, son-in-law of Philip Henslowe, was the leading spirit in the Lord Admiral's Men. Besides the adult companies, troupes of boy actors from time to time also enjoyed considerable popularity. Among these were the Children of Paul's and the Children of the Chapel Royal.

The company with which Shakespeare had a long association had for its first patron Henry Carey, Lord Hunsdon, the Lord Chamberlain, and hence they were known as the Lord Chamberlain's Men. After the accession of James I, they became the King's Men. This company was the great rival of the Lord Admiral's Men, managed by Henslowe and Alleyn.

All was not easy for the players in Shakespeare's time, for the aldermen of London were always eager for an excuse to close up the Blackfriars and any other theatres in their jurisdiction. The theatres outside the jurisdiction of London were not immune from interference, for they might be shut up by order of the Privy Council for meddling in politics or for various other offenses, or they might be closed in time of plague lest they spread infection. During plague times, the actors usually went on tour and played the provinces wherever they could find an audience. Particularly frightening were the plagues of 1592–1594 and 1613 when the theatres closed and the players, like many other Londoners, had to take to the country.

Though players had a low social status, they enjoyed great popularity, and one of the favorite forms of entertainment at Court was the performance of plays. To be commanded to perform at Court conferred great prestige upon a company of players, and printers frequently noted that fact when they published plays. Several of Shakespeare's plays were performed before the sovereign, and Shakespeare himself undoubtedly acted in some of these plays.

REFERENCES FOR FURTHER READING

Many readers will want suggestions for further reading about Shakespeare and his times. A few references will serve as guides to further study in the enormous literature on the subject. A simple and useful little book is Gerald Sanders, *A Shakespeare Primer* (New York, 1950). *A Companion to Shakespeare Studies,* edited by Harley Granville-Barker and G. B. Harrison (Cambridge, 1934), is a valuable guide. The most recent concise handbook of facts about Shakespeare is Gerald E. Bentley, *Shakespeare: A Biographical Handbook* (New Haven, 1961). More detailed but not so voluminous as to be confusing is Hazelton Spencer, *The Art and Life of William Shakespeare* (New York, 1940), which, like Sanders' and Bentley's handbooks, contains a brief annotated list of useful books on various aspects of the subject. The most detailed and scholarly work providing complete factual information about Shakespeare is Sir Edmund Chambers, *William Shakespeare: A Study of Facts and Problems* (2 vols., Oxford, 1930).

Among other biographies of Shakespeare, Joseph Quincy Adams, *A Life of William Shakespeare* (Boston, 1923) is still an excellent assessment of the essential facts and the traditional information, and Marchette Chute, *Shakespeare of London* (New York, 1949; paperback, 1957) stresses Shakespeare's life in the theatre. Two new biographies of Shakespeare have recently appeared. A. L. Rowse, *William Shakespeare: A Biography* (London, 1963; New York, 1964) provides an appraisal by a distinguished English historian, who dismisses the notion that somebody else wrote Shakespeare's plays as arrant nonsense that runs counter to known historical fact. Peter Quennell, *Shakespeare: A Biography* (Cleveland and New York, 1963) is a sensitive and intelligent survey of what is known and surmised of Shakespeare's life. Louis B. Wright, *Shakespeare for Everyman* (paperback; New York, 1964) discusses the basis of Shakespeare's enduring popularity.

The Shakespeare Quarterly, published by the Shakespeare Association of America under the editorship of James G. McManaway, is recommended for those who wish to keep up with current Shakespearean scholarship and stage productions. The *Quarterly* includes an annual bibliography of Shakespeare editions and works on Shakespeare published during the previous year.

The question of the authenticity of Shakespeare's plays arouses perennial attention. The theory of hidden cryptograms in the plays is demolished by William F. and Elizebeth S. Friedman, *The Shakespearean Ciphers Examined* (New York, 1957). A succinct account of the various absurdities advanced to suggest the authorship of a multitude of candidates other than Shakespeare will be found in R. C. Churchill, *Shakespeare and His Betters* (Bloomington, Ind., 1959). Another recent discussion of the subject, *The Authorship of Shakespeare,* by James G. McManaway (Washington, D.C., 1962), presents the evidence from contemporary records to prove the identity of Shakespeare the actor-playwright with Shakespeare of Stratford.

Scholars are not in agreement about the details of playhouse construction in the Elizabethan period. John C. Adams presents a plausible reconstruction of the Globe in *The Globe Playhouse: Its Design and Equipment* (Cambridge, Mass., 1942; 2nd rev. ed., 1961). A description with excellent drawings based on Dr. Adams' model is Irwin Smith, *Shakespeare's Globe Playhouse: A Modern Reconstruction in Text and Scale Drawings* (New York, 1956). Other sensible discussions are C. Walter Hodges, *The Globe Restored* (London, 1953) and A. M. Nagler, *Shakespeare's Stage* (New Haven, 1958). Bernard Beckerman, *Shakespeare at the Globe, 1599–1609* (New Haven, 1962; paperback, 1962) discusses Elizabethan staging and acting techniques.

A sound and readable history of the early theatres is Joseph Quincy Adams, *Shakespearean Playhouses: A History of English Theatres from the Beginnings to the Restoration* (Boston, 1917). For detailed, factual information about the Elizabethan and seventeenth-century stages, the definitive reference works are Sir Edmund Chambers, *The Elizabethan*

Stage (4 vols., Oxford, 1923) and Gerald E. Bentley, *The Jacobean and Caroline Stages* (5 vols., Oxford, 1941–1956).

Further information on the history of the theatre and related topics will be found in the following titles: T. W. Baldwin, *The Organization and Personnel of the Shakespearean Company* (Princeton, 1927); Lily Bess Campbell, *Scenes and Machines on the English Stage during the Renaissance* (Cambridge, 1923); Esther Cloudman Dunn, *Shakespeare in America* (New York, 1939); George C. D. Odell, *Shakespeare from Betterton to Irving* (2 vols., London, 1931); Arthur Colby Sprague, *Shakespeare and the Actors: The Stage Business in His Plays (1660–1905)* (Cambridge, Mass., 1944) and *Shakespearian Players and Performances* (Cambridge, Mass., 1953); Leslie Hotson, *The Commonwealth and Restoration Stage* (Cambridge, Mass, 1928); Alwin Thaler, *Shakspere to Sheridan: A Book about the Theatre of Yesterday and To-day* (Cambridge Mass., 1922); George C. Branam, *Eighteenth-Century Adaptations of Shakespeare's Tragedies* (Berkeley, 1956); C. Beecher Hogan, *Shakespeare in the Theatre, 1701–1800* (Oxford, 1957); Ernest Bradlee Watson, *Sheridan to Robertson: A Study of the 19th-Century London Stage* (Cambridge, Mass., 1926); and Enid Welsford, *The Court Masque* (Cambridge, Mass., 1927).

A brief account of the growth of Shakespeare's reputation is F. E. Halliday, *The Cult of Shakespeare* (London, 1947). A more detailed discussion

is given in Augustus Ralli, *A History of Shakespearian Criticism* (2 vols., Oxford, 1932; New York,
1958). Harley Granville-Barker, *Prefaces to Shakespeare* (5 vols., London, 1927–1948; 2 vols., London,
1958) provides stimulating critical discussion of the
plays. An older classic of criticism is Andrew C.
Bradley, *Shakespearean Tragedy: Lectures on Hamlet, Othello, King Lear, Macbeth* (London, 1904;
paperback, 1955). Sir Edmund Chambers, *Shakespeare: A Survey* (London, 1935; paperback, 1958)
contains short, sensible essays on thirty-four of the
plays, originally written as introductions to single-
play editions.

For the history plays see Lily Bess Campbell,
*Shakespeare's "Histories": Mirrors of Elizabethan
Policy* (Cambridge, 1947); John Palmer, *Political
Characters of Shakespeare* (London, 1945; 1961);
E. M. W. Tillyard, *Shakespeare's History Plays*
(London, 1948); Irving Ribner, *The English History
Play in the Age of Shakespeare* (Princeton, 1947);
and Max M. Reese, *The Cease of Majesty* (London,
1961).

The comedies are illuminated by the follow-
ing studies: C. L. Barber, *Shakespeare's Festive
Comedy* (Princeton, 1959); John Russell Brown,
Shakespeare and His Comedies (London, 1957);
H. B. Charlton, *Shakespearian Comedy* (London,
1938; 4th ed., 1949); W. W. Lawrence, *Shake-
speare's Problem Comedies* (New York, 1931); and
Thomas M. Parrott, *Shakespearean Comedy* (New
York, 1949).

The most recent study of *The Merry Wives of Windsor*, which considers the problem of dating in detail and offers convincing argument for 1597, is William Green, *Shakespeare's Merry Wives of Windsor* (Princeton, 1962). Leslie Hotson, *Shakespeare versus Shallow* (Boston, 1931) presents the thesis that Justice Shallow was intended as a satire on a notorious Surrey justice against whom Shakespeare had a grievance. Further discussion of the problem of the text and the incomplete horse-stealing subplot is to be found in William Bracy, *The Merry Wives of Windsor. The History and Transmission of Shakespeare's Text* (Columbia, Mo., 1952) and John E. V. Crofts, *Shakespeare and the Post Horses* (Bristol, 1937). The dating of *The Merry Wives of Windsor* and the play's relation to *Henry IV, Parts 1* and *2* and *Henry V* are also discussed by Arthur R. Humphreys in his edition of *The First Part of King Henry IV* for the Arden series (London, 1960).

Further discussions of Shakespeare's tragedies, in addition to Bradley, already cited, are contained in H. B. Charlton, *Shakespearian Tragedy* (Cambridge, 1948); Willard Farnham, *The Medieval Heritage of Elizabethan Tragedy* (Berkeley, 1936) and *Shakespeare's Tragic Frontier: The World of His Final Tragedies* (Berkeley, 1950); and Harold S. Wilson, *On the Design of Shakespearian Tragedy* (Toronto, 1957).

The "Roman" plays are treated in M. M. MacCallum, *Shakespeare's Roman Plays and Their Back-*

ground (London, 1910) and J. C. Maxwell, "Shakespeare's Roman Plays, 1900–1956," *Shakespeare Survey 10* (Cambridge, 1957), 1-11.

Kenneth Muir, *Shakespeare's Sources: Comedies and Tragedies* (London, 1957) discusses Shakespeare's use of source material. The sources themselves have been reprinted several times. Among old editions are John P. Collier (ed.), *Shakespeare's Library* (2 vols., London, 1850), Israel C. Gollancz (ed.), *The Shakespeare Classics* (12 vols., London, 1907–26), and W. C. Hazlitt (ed.), *Shakespeare's Library* (6 vols., London, 1875). A modern edition is being prepared by Geoffrey Bullough with the title *Narrative and Dramatic Sources of Shakespeare* (London and New York, 1957–). Four volumes, covering the sources for the comedies and histories, have been published to date (1964).

In addition to the second edition of *Webster's New International Dictionary*, which contains most of the unusual words used by Shakespeare, the following reference works are helpful: Edwin A. Abbott, *A Shakespearian Grammar* (London, 1872); C. T. Onions, *A Shakespeare Glossary* (2nd rev. ed., Oxford, 1925); and Eric Partridge, *Shakespeare's Bawdy* (New York, 1948; paperback, 1960).

Some knowledge of the social background of the period in which Shakespeare lived is important for a full understanding of his work. A brief, clear, and accurate account of Tudor history is S. T. Bindoff, *The Tudors*, in the Penguin series. A readable general history is G. M. Trevelyan, *The History of Eng-*

land, first published in 1926 and available in numerous editions. The same author's *English Social History,* first published in 1942 and also available in many editions, provides fascinating information about England in all periods. Sir John Neale, *Queen Elizabeth* (London, 1935; paperback, 1957) is the best study of the great Queen. Various aspects of life in the Elizabethan period are treated in Louis B. Wright, *Middle-Class Culture in Elizabethan England* (Chapel Hill, N.C., 1935; reprinted Ithaca, N.Y., 1958, 1964). *Shakespeare's England: An Account of the Life and Manners of His Age,* edited by Sidney Lee and C. T. Onions (2 vols., Oxford, 1917), provides much information on many aspects of Elizabethan life. A fascinating survey of the period will be found in Muriel St. C. Byrne, *Elizabethan Life in Town and Country* (London, 1925; rev. ed., 1954; paperback, 1961).

The Folger Library is issuing a series of illustrated booklets entitled "Folger Booklets on Tudor and Stuart Civilization," printed and distributed by Cornell University Press. Published to date are the following titles:

D. W. Davies, *Dutch Influences on English Culture, 1558-1625*

Giles E. Dawson, *The Life of William Shakespeare*

Ellen C. Eyler, *Early English Gardens and Garden Books*

John R. Hale, *The Art of War and Renaissance England*

William Haller, *Elizabeth I and the Puritans*

Virginia A. LaMar, *English Dress in the Age of Shakespeare*

————, *Travel and Roads in England*

John L. Lievsay, *The Elizabethan Image of Italy*

James G. McManaway, *The Authorship of Shakespeare*

Dorothy E. Mason, *Music in Elizabethan England*

Garrett Mattingly, *The "Invincible" Armada and Elizabethan England*

Boies Penrose, *Tudor and Early Stuart Voyaging*

Conyers Read, *The Government of England under Elizabeth*

Albert J. Schmidt, *The Yeoman in Tudor and Stuart England*

Lilly C. Stone, *English Sports and Recreations*

Craig R. Thompson, *The Bible in English, 1525–1611*

————, *The English Church in the Sixteenth Century*

————, *Schools in Tudor England*

————, *Universities in Tudor England*

Louis B. Wright, *Shakespeare's Theatre and the Dramatic Tradition*

At intervals the Folger Library plans to gather these booklets in hardbound volumes. The first is *Life and Letters in Tudor and Stuart England, First Folger Series*, edited by Louis B. Wright and Virginia A. LaMar (published for the Folger Shakespeare Library by Cornell University Press, 1962). The volume contains eleven of the separate booklets.

[Dramatis Personae

Sir John Falstaff.
Fenton, a gentleman.
Shallow, a country justice.
Abraham Slender, cousin to *Shallow*.
Ford, } two gentlemen dwelling at Windsor.
Page,
William Page, a boy, son to *Page*.
Sir Hugh Evans, a Welsh parson.
Doctor Caius, a French physician.
Host of the Garter Inn.
Bardolph,
Pistol, } sharpers attending on Falstaff.
Nym,
Robin, page to *Falstaff*.
Simple, servant to *Slender*.
Jack Rugby, servant to *Doctor Caius*.
Mistress Ford.
Mistress Page.
Anne Page, her daughter.
Mistress Quickly, servant to *Doctor Caius*.

Servants to Page, Ford, etc.

Scene: *Windsor, and the neighborhood.*]

THE
MERRY WIVES
OF
WINDSOR

ACT I

I.i. Justice Shallow complains to his cousin, Abraham Slender, and Sir Hugh Evans, a Welsh clergyman, of his injuries at the hands of Sir John Falstaff. Evans counsels him to forget his grievances and seek the hand of Anne Page for Slender. At Page's house they find Falstaff, who impudently admits the wrongs he has done Justice Shallow but is unrepentant. Slender is talked into agreeing to court Anne Page and has a few halting words with her before they join the rest of the company at dinner.

<hr/>

1. **Sir Hugh:** the title **Sir,** deriving from the Latin *dominus* earned by those who took a bachelor's degree, indicates that he is a clergyman.

1–2. **a Star Chamber matter:** the Court of Star Chamber, composed of the Privy Council and the Chief Justices of the Queen's Bench and the Common Pleas, dealt largely with disturbances of the public peace and with cases of slander and libel.

5. **coram:** i.e., "of the quorum," meaning one of the justices whose presence was necessary before certain sorts of cases could be decided.

6. **custalorum:** *custos rotulorum*, keeper of the county records, usually also the presiding justice and a person of considerable local importance.

7. **ratolorum:** Slender's error for *rotulorum*.

8. **armigero:** *armiger*, a heraldic term for an esquire, one entitled to have a coat of arms.

14. **give:** i.e., display in their coats of arms; **luces:** the coat of the Lucy family of Charlecote was known

(continued on next page)

ACT I

Scene I. [Windsor. Before Page's house.]

Enter Justice Shallow, Slender, and Sir Hugh Evans.

Shal. Sir Hugh, persuade me not: I will make a Star
Chamber matter of it. If he were twenty Sir John Fal-
staffs, he shall not abuse Robert Shallow, Esquire.

Slen. In the county of Gloucester, justice of peace
and "coram."   5

Shal. Ay, cousin Slender, and *custalorum.*

Slen. Ay, and *ratolorum* too; and a gentleman born,
Master Parson, who writes himself *armigero,* in any
bill, warrant, quittance, or obligation, *armigero.*

Shal. Ay, that I do, and have done any time these   10
three hundred years.

Slen. All his successors gone before him hath done't;
and all his ancestors that come after him may. They
may give the dozen white luces in their coat.

Shal. It is an old coat.   15

Evans. The dozen white louses do become an old
coat well. It agrees well, passant: it is a familiar beast
to man and signifies love.

Shal. The luce is the fresh fish. The salt fish is an old
coat.   20

I

to contain **luces,** which led to the identification of Shallow with Sir Thomas Lucy. It was conjectured that Shakespeare satirized Lucy in retaliation for Lucy's severe reaction when he caught Shakespeare poaching his deer—a legend of Shakespeare's youth never confirmed nor completely dispelled.

17. **passant:** a heraldic term for "walking," that is, in motion.

19. **luce:** as Shallow points out, a luce is a fish, not the parasite with which Sir Hugh identifies it.

19–20. **The salt fish is an old coat:** a reference to the coat of arms of the Saltfishmongers' Company, an older coat than that of the Stockfishmongers, which bore luces. There is also a pun on *saltant* (leaping), which Shallow suggests as the correct term rather than Sir Hugh's **passant.**

❋   ❋   ❋

21. **quarter:** add another coat to his own by marrying a woman who also has a coat of arms. The two family arms would be "quartered" on the same shield to form their new coat.

25. **py'r Lady:** by our Lady (the Virgin).

26. **three skirts:** the portion of the garment below the waist was split into four sections.

27. **all one:** of no importance.

31. **Council:** Privy Council.

32. **meet:** fitting.

33. **Got:** Shakespeare represents a Welsh dialect by changing final *d* to *t* and often *b* to *p*.

35. **Take your vizaments in that:** i.e., be as-

(continued on next page)

2

Slen. I may quarter, coz.

Shal. You may, by marrying.

Evans. It is marring indeed, if he quarter it.

Shal. Not a whit.

Evans. Yes, py'r Lady: if he has a quarter of your 25
coat, there is but three skirts for yourself, in my simple conjectures; but that is all one. If Sir John Falstaff
have committed disparagements unto you, I am of the
church and will be glad to do my benevolence to
make atonements and compromises between you. 30

Shal. The Council shall hear it; it is a riot.

Evans. It is not meet the Council hear a riot: there
is no fear of Got in a riot. The Council, look you, shall
desire to hear the fear of Got, and not to hear a riot.
Take your vizaments in that. 35

Shal. Ha! o' my life, if I were young again, the
sword should end it.

Evans. It is petter that friends is the sword and end
it: and there is also another device in my prain, which
peradventure prings goot discretions with it. There is 40
Anne Page, which is daughter to Master Thomas
Page, which is pretty virginity.

Slen. Mistress Anne Page? She has brown hair and
speaks small like a woman.

Evans. It is that fery person for all the orld, as just 45
as you will desire; and seven hundred pounds of
moneys, and gold and silver, is her grandsire upon
his death's bed (Got deliver to a joyful resurrections!)
give, when she is able to overtake seventeen years
old. It were a goot motion if we leave our pribbles 50

sured of that fact. **Vizaments** means "advisements."

41–2. **Thomas Page:** since Page is addressed as George by his wife at II.i.149 and 157, an error has been made either by Shakespeare or the First Folio printer.

44. **small:** gently.

50–1. **pribbles and prabbles:** petty quarrels.

* * *

58. **gifts:** natural endowments.

59. **possibilities:** expectations of inheriting more money.

72. **tell you another tale:** i.e., discuss another matter (a suit for the hand of Anne Page).

The luces on the left of this coat of arms appear in the Lucy coat. From John Ferne, *The Blazon of Gentry* (1586).

and prabbles and desire a marriage between Master
Abraham and Mistress Anne Page.

Slen. Did her grandsire leave her seven hundred
pound?

Evans. Ay, and her father is make her a petter   55
penny.

Slen. I know the young gentlewoman. She has good
gifts.

Evans. Seven hundred pounds and possibilities is
goot gifts.   60

Shal. Well, let us see honest Master Page. Is Falstaff
there?

Evans. Shall I tell you a lie? I do despise a liar as I
do despise one that is false, or as I despise one that is
not true. The knight, Sir John, is there; and I beseech   65
you, be ruled by your well-willers. I will peat the door
for Master Page. [*Knocks.*] What, hoa! Got pless your
house here!

Page. [*Within*] Who's there?

[*Enter Page.*]

Evans. Here is Got's plessing, and your friend, and   70
Justice Shallow; and here young Master Slender, that
peradventures shall tell you another tale, if matters
grow to your likings.

Page. I am glad to see your Worships well. I thank
you for my venison, Master Shallow.   75

Shal. Master Page, I am glad to see you; much good
do it your good heart! I wished your venison better:

78. **ill killed:** killed illegally (perhaps referring to the deer Falstaff is said to have killed in lines 105–6).

84. **Cotsall:** i.e., in the Cotswold Hills. The dog was presumably outrun coursing hares.

87. **fault:** misfortune; i.e., only bad luck, since the dog is a good one.

100. **At a word:** in brief; to be short.

Coursing the hare.
From John Speed, *A Prospect of the Most Famous Parts of the World* (1631).

it was ill killed. How doth good Mistress Page?—and
I thank you always with my heart, la! with my heart.

   Page. Sir, I thank you.   80

   Shal. Sir, I thank you: by yea and no, I do.

   Page. I am glad to see you, good Master Slender.

   Slen. How does your fallow greyhound, sir? I heard
say he was outrun on Cotsall.

   Page. It could not be judged, sir.   85

   Slen. You'll not confess, you'll not confess.

   Shal. That he will not. 'Tis your fault, 'tis your fault;
'tis a good dog.

   Page. A cur, sir.

   Shal. Sir, he's a good dog, and a fair dog: can there 90
be more said? He is good and fair. Is Sir John Falstaff
here?

   Page. Sir, he is within; and I would I could do a
good office between you.

   Evans. It is spoke as a Christians ought to speak. 95

   Shal. He hath wronged me, Master Page.

   Page. Sir, he doth in some sort confess it.

   Shal. If it be confessed, it is not redressed. Is not
that so, Master Page? He hath wronged me, indeed he
hath. At a word, he hath, believe me: Robert Shallow, 100
Esquire, saith he is wronged.

   Page. Here comes Sir John.

[Enter Sir John Falstaff, Bardolph, Nym, and Pistol.]

   Fal. Now, Master Shallow, you'll complain of me to
the King?

108. **pin:** trifle; **answered:** atoned or paid for.

109. **straight:** immediately.

112–13. **known in counsel:** kept secret.

114. **Pauca verba:** few words; **worts:** words.

115. **worts:** plants of the cabbage family.

117. **Marry:** verily.

118. **cony-catching:** cheating.

121. **Banbury cheese:** a reference to Slender's physique. Banbury cheese was made in small forms that reduced to thin slices when the rind was pared off.

125. **Slice:** prompted by the reference to Banbury cheese, Nym threatens to slice Slender.

131. **fidelicet:** Latin *videlicet:* "that is to say."

Shal. Knight, you have beaten my men, killed my 105
deer, and broke open my lodge.

Fal. But not kissed your keeper's daughter?

Shal. Tut, a pin! this shall be answered.

Fal. I will answer it straight: I have done all this.
That is now answered.   110

Shal. The Council shall know this.

Fal. 'Twere better for you if it were known in counsel: you'll be laughed at.

Evans. Pauca verba, Sir John; good worts.

Fal. Good worts! good cabbage. Slender, I broke 115
your head. What matter have you against me?

Slen. Marry, sir, I have matter in my head against
you, and against your cony-catching rascals, Bardolph, Nym, and Pistol. They carried me to the tavern
and made me drunk, and afterward picked my pocket. 120

Bar. You Banbury cheese!

Slen. Ay, it is no matter.

Pis. How now, Mephistophilus!

Slen. Ay, it is no matter.

Nym. Slice, I say; *Pauca, pauca*: slice! that's my 125
humor.

Slen. Where's Simple, my man? Can you tell, cousin?

Evans. Peace, I pray you. Now let us understand.
There is three umpires in this matter, as I under- 130
stand: that is, Master Page, *fidelicet* Master Page; and
there is myself, *fidelicet* myself; and the three party is,
lastly and finally, mine host of the Garter.

145. **groats:** coins worth fourpence each; **mill-sixpences:** sixpences with milled edges.

145–46. **Edward shovelboards:** shillings of the coinage of Edward VI, which were used in the game called shovelboard.

149. **false:** dishonest.

150. **mountain-foreigner:** a contemptuous term for a Welshman.

152. **latten bilbo:** sword made of a thin sheet of soft metal and therefore not very dangerous. Pistol probably also puns on "lathen," made of lathe, and part of the insult has reference to Slender's lean body.

153. **labras:** lips (Latin *labrum*).

156. **Be avised:** take care.

157. **say "marry trap":** a term of dubious meaning but implying a threat. The exclamation **marry** is often used with nonsense words.

157–58. **run the nuthook's humor on me:** threaten me with arrest. **Nuthook** was another term for a constable.

162. **Scarlet and John:** Will Scarlet and Little John, the companions of Robin Hood. **Scarlet** is Bardolph of the red face.

Page. We three to hear it and end it between them.

Evans. Fery goot: I will make a prief of it in my   135
notebook, and we will afterwards ork upon the cause
with as great discreetly as we can.

Fal. Pistol!

Pis. He hears with ears.

Evans. The tevil and his tam! what phrase is this,   140
"He hears with ear"? Why, it is affectations.

Fal. Pistol, did you pick Master Slender's purse?

Slen. Ay, by these gloves, did he, or I would I might
never come in mine own great chamber again else, of
seven groats in mill-sixpences, and two Edward   145
shovelboards, that cost me two shilling and twopence
apiece of Yead Miller, by these gloves.

Fal. Is this true, Pistol?

Evans. No, it is false, if it is a pickpurse.

Pis. Ha, thou mountain-foreigner! Sir John and   150
    master mine,
I combat challenge of this latten bilbo.
Word of denial in thy *labras* here!
Word of denial: froth and scum, thou liest!

Slen. By these gloves, then, 'twas he.   155

Nym. Be avised, sir, and pass good humors: I will
say "marry trap" with you, if you run the nuthook's
humor on me. That is the very note of it.

Slen. By this hat, then, he in the red face had it; for
though I cannot remember what I did when you made   160
me drunk, yet I am not altogether an ass.

Fal. What say you, Scarlet and John?

167. **fap:** drunk; **cashiered:** robbed.

168. **conclusions passed the careers:** to "pass a career" meant to execute a full gallop on horseback. Bardolph simply means "the matter was concluded."

S.D. 176. **Mistress Ford:** the title **Mistress** was applied to married and unmarried women alike.

187. **Book of Songs and Sonnets:** a collection of verse brought together by Richard Tottel (1557), often known as "Tottel's Miscellany."

En lapis, in medio qui tendit ad exteriora
Appositum sumens pocla meretur ovans.

Wer in der Mitt schickt vist zu End
Mit seinem Stain der kriegt behendt
Die Zeche frey vnd nimbt hinweg
Was zugesetzt auf diesem Zweg

Playing shovelboard.
From *Le centre de l'amour* (ca. 1600).

Bar. Why, sir, for my part, I say the gentleman had
drunk himself out of his five sentences.

Evans. It is his five senses: fie, what the ignorance 165
is!

Bar. And being fap, sir, was, as they say, cashiered;
and so conclusions passed the careers.

Slen. Ay, you spake in Latin then too; but 'tis no
matter: I'll ne'er be drunk whilst I live again but in 170
honest, civil, godly company, for this trick. If I be
drunk, I'll be drunk with those that have the fear of
God, and not with drunken knaves.

Evans. So Got udge me, that is a virtuous mind.

Fal. You hear all these matters denied, gentlemen; 175
you hear it.

[*Enter Anne Page, with wine; Mistress Ford and
Mistress Page, following.*]

Page. Nay, daughter, carry the wine in; we'll drink
within.   [*Exit Anne Page.*]

Slen. O heaven! this is Mistress Anne Page.

Page. How now, Mistress Ford!   180

Fal. Mistress Ford, by my troth, you are very well
met. By your leave, good mistress. *Sir John kisses her.*

Page. Wife, bid these gentlemen welcome. Come,
we have a hot venison pasty to dinner. Come, gentlemen, I hope we shall drink down all unkindness.   185

[*Exeunt all except Shallow, Slender, and Evans*]

Slen. I had rather than forty shillings I had my
Book of Songs and Sonnets here.

189. **Book of Riddles:** books of riddles were popular and were frequently read out of existence. It is impossible to identify the particular collection that Slender mentions.

192. **Allhallowmas:** All Saints' Day, November 1.

193. **Michaelmas:** September 29. This is presumably intended to be Simple's error.

194. **coz:** a term loosely applied to various near relatives.

196. **tender:** offer.

202. **motions:** proposals.

203. **capacity:** capable of understanding.

207. **simple though I stand here:** i.e., as sure as I stand here; a common phrase.

[*Enter Simple.*]

How now, Simple! where have you been? I must wait
on myself, must I? You have not the *Book of Riddles*
about you, have you?   190

Sim. *Book of Riddles!* why, did you not lend it to
Alice Shortcake upon Allhallowmas last, a fortnight
afore Michaelmas?

Shal. Come, coz, come, coz: we stay for you. A word
with you, coz; marry, this, coz: there is, as 'twere, a   195
tender, a kind of tender, made afar off by Sir Hugh
here. Do you understand me?

Slen. Ay, sir, you shall find me reasonable. If it be
so, I shall do that that is reason.

Shal. Nay, but understand me.   200

Slen. So I do, sir.

Evans. Give ear to his motions. Master Slender, I
will description the matter to you, if you be capacity
of it.

Slen. Nay, I will do as my cousin Shallow says. I   205
pray you, pardon me: he's a justice of peace in his
country, simple though I stand here.

Evans. But that is not the question: the question is
concerning your marriage.

Shal. Ay, there's the point, sir.   210

Evans. Marry, is it, the very point of it, to Mistress
Anne Page.

Slen. Why, if it be so, I will marry her upon any
reasonable demands.

215. **affection:** affect; love.

215–16. **command:** demand.

217. **parcel:** part.

224. **possitable:** positively.

230. **conceive:** understand.

237–38. **I hope upon familiarity will grow more contempt:** the proverbial saying, "Familiarity breeds contempt." Slender means to say "content."

239. **dissolved:** resolved.

240. **fall:** fault.

Evans. But can you affection the oman? Let us com- 215
mand to know that of your mouth or of your lips: for
divers philosophers hold that the lips is parcel of the
mouth. Therefore, precisely, can you carry your good
will to the maid?

Shal. Cousin Abraham Slender, can you love her? 220

Slen. I hope, sir, I will do as it shall become one
that would do reason.

Evans. Nay, Got's lords and his ladies! you must
speak possitable, if you can carry her your desires
towards her. 225

Shal. That you must. Will you, upon good dowry,
marry her?

Slen. I will do a greater thing than that upon your
request, cousin, in any reason.

Shal. Nay, conceive me, conceive me, sweet coz. 230
What I do is to pleasure you, coz. Can you love the
maid?

Slen. I will marry her, sir, at your request; but if
there be no great love in the beginning, yet Heaven
may decrease it upon better acquaintance, when we 235
are married and have more occasion to know one another. I hope upon familiarity will grow more contempt: but if you say, "Marry her," I will marry her,
that I am freely dissolved, and dissolutely.

Evans. It is a fery discretion answer; save the fall is 240
in the ord "dissolutely": the ort is, according to our
meaning, "resolutely." His meaning is good.

Shal. Ay, I think my cousin meant well.

249. **wait on:** attend.

Slen. Ay, or else I would I might be hanged, la!

Shal. Here comes fair Mistress Anne.   245

[*Enter Anne Page.*]

Would I were young for your sake, Mistress Anne!

Anne. The dinner is on the table. My father desires
your Worships' company.

Shal. I will wait on him, fair Mistress Anne.

Evans. Od's plessed will! I will not be absence at   250
the grace.   [*Exeunt Shallow and Evans.*]

Anne. Will't please your Worship to come in, sir?

Slen. No, I thank you, forsooth, heartily: I am very
well.

Anne. The dinner attends you, sir.   255

Slen. I am not a-hungry, I thank you, forsooth. Go,
sirrah, for all you are my man, go wait upon my cousin Shallow. [*Exit Simple.*] A justice of peace sometime may be beholding to his friend for a man. I keep
but three men and a boy yet, till my mother be dead: 260
but what though? Yet I live like a poor gentleman
born.

Anne. I may not go in without your Worship: they
will not sit till you come.

Slen. I' faith, I'll eat nothing. I thank you as much   265
as though I did.

Anne. I pray you, sir, walk in.

Slen. I had rather walk here, I thank you. I bruised
my shin the other day with playing at sword and dag-

270. **veneys:** venues; thrusts, or bouts.

271. **stewed prunes:** a dish associated with brothels.

280. **Sackerson:** a famous bear that performed in the Bear Garden on the Bankside.

282. **it passed:** i.e., it surpassed anything.

288. **cock and pie:** a mild oath.

Fencing with sword and dagger.
From Giacomo di Grassi, *True Art of Defense* (1594).

ger with a master of fence (three veneys for a dish of 270
stewed prunes) and, by my troth, I cannot abide the
smell of hot meat since. Why do your dogs bark so?
Be there bears i' the town?

Anne. I think there are, sir. I heard them talked of.

Slen. I love the sport well, but I shall as soon quar- 275
rel at it as any man in England. You are afraid, if you
see the bear loose, are you not?

Anne. Ay, indeed, sir.

Slen. That's meat and drink to me, now. I have seen
Sackerson loose twenty times, and have taken him by 280
the chain; but, I warrant you, the women have so
cried and shrieked at it that it passed. But women, indeed, cannot abide 'em: they are very ill-favored
rough things.

[*Enter Page.*]

Page. Come, gentle Master Slender, come. We stay 285
for you.

Slen. I'll eat nothing, I thank you, sir.

Page. By cock and pie, you shall not choose, sir!
Come, come!

Slen. Nay, pray you, lead the way. 290

Page. Come on, sir.

Slen. Mistress Anne, yourself shall go first.

Anne. Not I, sir: pray you, keep on.

Slen. Truly, I will not go first: truly, la! I will not
do you that wrong. 295

Anne. I pray you, sir.

I.ii. Evans sends Slender's man, Simple, with a message to Mrs. Quickly to urge her support for Slender's suit to Anne Page.

‖‖‖‖‖‖‖‖‖‖‖‖‖‖‖‖‖‖‖‖‖‖‖‖‖‖‖‖‖‖‖

1–2. ask of Doctor Caius' house which is the way: i.e., ask the way to Doctor Caius' house.

‖‖‖‖‖‖‖‖‖‖‖‖‖‖‖‖‖‖‖‖‖‖‖‖‖‖‖‖‖‖‖

I.iii. Falstaff tells the host of the Garter Inn that his expenses are too heavy and he must discharge some followers. The host offers to hire Bardolph as a tapster. Falstaff then discloses a plan to make love to Mrs. Ford. He thinks she has shown him particular favor and hopes to enrich himself from her husband's purse. At the same time, he imagines that Mrs. Page is similarly enamored of him; she shows promise of being another source of money. When both Pistol and Nym refuse to deliver letters to the two women, Falstaff gives them to Robin, his page, and orders his erstwhile followers to go shift for themselves. Nym and Pistol resolve to warn Ford and Page of Falstaff's designs on their wives.

Slen. I'll rather be unmannerly than troublesome.
You do yourself wrong, indeed, la!

Exeunt.

Scene II. [Before Page's house.]

Enter [Sir Hugh] Evans and Simple.

Evans. Go your ways and ask of Doctor Caius'
house which is the way: and there dwells one Mistress
Quickly, which is in the manner of his nurse, or his
dry nurse, or his cook, or his laundry, his washer, and
his wringer.   5

Sim. Well, sir.

Evans. Nay, it is petter yet. Give her this letter; for
it is a oman that altogether's acquaintance with Mistress Anne Page; and the letter is to desire and require
her to solicit your master's desires to Mistress Anne   10
Page. I pray you, be gone. I will make an end of my
dinner: there's pippins and cheese to come.

Exeunt.

Scene III. [A room in the Garter Inn.]

*Enter Falstaff, Host, Bardolph, Nym, Pistol, and
Robin.*

Fal. Mine host of the Garter!

2. **bullyrook:** boon companion; pal.

7. **wag:** be off.

8. **I sit at ten pounds a week:** i.e., my living expenses are ten pounds a week.

10. **Pheezar:** probably, "vizier;" **entertain:** hire.

14. **froth and lime:** serve frothing ale and limed (adulterated) sack; **I am at a word:** i.e., I am a man of few words; that settles it.

17. **An old cloak makes a new jerkin:** proverbial.

20. **Hungarian wight:** beggar, deriving either from soldiers who begged for their living after returning from war in Hungary or from a popular notion that gypsies originated in Hungary.

22. **gotten:** begotten.

23. **conceited:** clever.

24. **acquit:** quit; **tinderbox:** another reference to Bardolph's red face.

26. **kept not time:** i.e., stole even when he was certain to be caught.

28. **fico:** fig, or fig of Spain.

Host. What says my bullyrook? Speak scholarly and
wisely.

Fal. Truly, mine host, I must turn away some of my
followers.   5

Host. Discard, bully Hercules: cashier. Let them
wag: trot, trot!

Fal. I sit at ten pounds a week.

Host. Thou'rt an emperor, Caesar, Keisar, and
Pheezar. I will entertain Bardolph: he shall draw, he   10
shall tap. Said I well, bully Hector?

Fal. Do so, good mine host.

Host. I have spoke: let him follow. [*To Bardolph.*]
Let me see thee froth and lime. I am at a word: fol-
low!   [*Exit.*]   15

Fal. Bardolph, follow him. A tapster is a good trade.
An old cloak makes a new jerkin, a withered serving-
man a fresh tapster. Go; adieu.

Bar. It is a life that I have desired: I will thrive.

Pis. O base Hungarian wight! wilt thou the spigot   20
wield?   [*Exit Bardolph.*]

Nym. He was gotten in drink: is not the humor
conceited?

Fal. I am glad I am so acquit of this tinderbox. His
thefts were too open; his filching was like an unskillful   25
singer: he kept not time.

Nym. The good humor is to steal at a minute's rest.

Pis. "Convey," the wise it call. "Steal"! foh! a fico
for the phrase!

Fal. Well, sirs, I am almost out at heels.   30

31. **kibes:** chilblains.

33. **shift:** use tricks.

42. **entertainment:** ready welcome.

43. **carves:** shows partiality (from carving the choicest bits for a favored guest).

43–4. **construe the action of her familiar style:** interpret her familiar manner, with a pun on the grammatical sense of the phrase.

44. **hardest voice:** most certain interpretation.

45. **Englished:** expressed in plain English.

48. **will:** a pun on the sense "carnal desire"; **honesty:** chastity.

49. **The anchor is deep:** it's a deep-laid plot.

51. **angels:** coins of ten shillings' value each.

52. **As many devils entertain:** enlist as many devils to help you.

59. **oeillades:** ogles.

Pis. Why, then, let kibes ensue.

Fal. There is no remedy: I must cony-catch, I must shift.

Pis. Young ravens must have food.

Fal. Which of you know Ford of this town?   35

Pis. I ken the wight: he is of substance good.

Fal. My honest lads, I will tell you what I am about.

Pis. Two yards and more.

Fal. No quips now, Pistol! Indeed, I am in the waist two yards about; but I am now about no waste: I am   40 about thrift. Briefly, I do mean to make love to Ford's wife. I spy entertainment in her: she discourses, she carves, she gives the leer of invitation. I can construe the action of her familiar style, and the hardest voice of her behavior, to be Englished rightly, is, "I am Sir   45 John Falstaff's."

Pis. He hath studied her well and translated her will out of honesty into English.

Nym. The anchor is deep: will that humor pass?

Fal. Now, the report goes she has all the rule of her   50 husband's purse: he hath a legion of angels.

Pis. As many devils entertain! And "To her, boy," say I.

Nym. The humor rises; it is good. Humor me the angels.   55

Fal. I have writ me here a letter to her; and here another to Page's wife, who even now gave me good eyes too, examined my parts with most judicious oeillades. Sometimes the beam of her view gilded my foot, sometimes my portly belly.   60

61. Then did the sun on dunghill shine: referring to the proverb "The sun is never the worse for shining on a dunghill."

66–7. a region in Guiana: a reference to Sir Walter Raleigh's narrative, *The Discovery of the Large, Rich, and Beautiful Empire of Guiana* (1596), which inspired high hopes for that region as a source of gold.

68. cheaters: escheators, officers who handled the transfer to the Crown of escheated property, with a pun on the obvious meaning.

73. Pandarus: the uncle of Cressida, who assisted Troilus in his suit for her hand; the original pander.

78. tightly: quickly and safely.

83. French thrift: i.e., follow the French fashion of dismissing all of his servants but one page; **skirted:** dressed in a livery with skirts instead of doublet and hose.

84–5. gourd and fullam: two types of loaded dice.

87. Tester: teston, a sixpence.

Pis. Then did the sun on dunghill shine.

Nym. I thank thee for that humor.

Fal. O, she did so course o'er my exteriors, with
such a greedy intention, that the appetite of her eye
did seem to scorch me up like a burning glass! Here's   65
another letter to her: she bears the purse too. She is a
region in Guiana, all gold and bounty. I will be
cheaters to them both, and they shall be exchequers
to me. They shall be my East and West Indies and I
will trade to them both. Go bear thou this letter to   70
Mistress Page; and thou this to Mistress Ford. We will
thrive, lads, we will thrive.

Pis. Shall I Sir Pandarus of Troy become
And by my side wear steel? Then, Lucifer take all!

Nym. I will run no base humor. Here, take the hu-   75
mor-letter: I will keep the havior of reputation.

Fal. [*To Robin*] Hold, sirrah, bear you these letters
    tightly.
Sail like my pinnace to these golden shores!
Rogues, hence, avaunt! vanish like hailstones, go!   80
Trudge, plod away o' the hoof; seek shelter, pack!
Falstaff will learn the humor of the age,
French thrift, you rogues: myself and skirted page.
                    [*Exeunt Falstaff and Robin.*]

Pis. Let vultures gripe thy guts! for gourd and
    fullam holds,   85
And high and low beguiles the rich and poor.
Tester I'll have in pouch when thou shalt lack,
Base Phrygian Turk!

92. **welkin and her star:** heaven and the sun.
101–2. **yellowness:** jealousy; **the revolt of mine:** my rebellion against Falstaff.

◼◼◼◼◼◼◼◼◼◼◼◼◼◼◼◼◼◼◼◼◼◼◼◼◼◼◼◼◼◼

I.iv. Simple's visit to Quickly is interrupted by the return of Dr. Caius. When he is told the nature of Simple's errand, Dr. Caius, who also loves Anne Page, writes Evans a challenge. After Caius has departed for the court, Fenton enters and reveals himself as yet another suitor for Anne Page. To his face Mrs. Quickly encourages his hopes, but she has private doubts that he will succeed.

◼◼◼◼◼◼◼◼◼◼◼◼◼◼◼◼◼◼◼◼◼◼◼◼

4. **old:** extraordinary in degree.

Nym. I have operations which be humors of re-
venge.   90

Pis. Wilt thou revenge?

Nym. By welkin and her star!

Pis. With wit or steel?

Nym. With both the humors, I. I will discuss the
humor of this love to Page.   95

Pis. And I to Ford shall eke unfold
      How Falstaff, varlet vile,
   His dove will prove, his gold will hold,
    And his soft couch defile.

Nym. My humor shall not cool. I will incense Page 100
to deal with poison. I will possess him with yellowness, for the revolt of mine is dangerous: that is my
true humor.

Pis. Thou art the Mars of malcontents. I second
thee: troop on.   105

                          Exeunt.

Scene IV. [A room in Doctor Caius' house.]

Enter Mistress Quickly, Simple, and Rugby.

Quick. What, John Rugby! I pray thee, go to the
casement and see if you can see my master, Master
Doctor Caius, coming. If he do, i' faith, and find anybody in the house, here will be an old abusing of
God's patience and the King's English.   5

Rug. I'll go watch.

7. **posset:** a hot drink of curdled milk, usually laced with wine; **soon at night:** tonight.

8. **sea-coal:** made of coals brought by sea from Newcastle, so called to distinguish it from charcoal.

11. **breedbate:** troublemaker.

12. **something peevish:** somewhat silly.

21. **Cain-colored:** Robert Nares's *Glossary* defines the word as yellow or red "which being esteemed a deformity was by common consent attributed to Cain and Judas."

22. **softly-sprighted:** meek; timid.

23. **tall:** brave; **of:** with.

25. **warrener:** gamekeeper.

Quick. Go; and we'll have a posset for't soon at
night, in faith, at the latter end of a sea-coal fire.
[*Exit Rugby.*] An honest, willing, kind fellow, as ever
servant shall come in house withal; and, I warrant   10
you, no telltale nor no breedbate. His worst fault is
that he is given to prayer: he is something peevish
that way; but nobody but has his fault; but let that
pass. Peter Simple you say your name is?

Sim. Ay, for fault of a better.   15

Quick. And Master Slender's your master?

Sim. Ay, forsooth.

Quick. Does he not wear a great round beard, like
a glover's paring knife?

Sim. No, forsooth: he hath but a little wee face,   20
with a little yellow beard, a Cain-colored beard.

Quick. A softly-sprighted man, is he not?

Sim. Ay, forsooth; but he is as tall a man of his
hands as any is between this and his head: he hath
fought with a warrener.   25

Quick. How say you? O, I should remember him:
does he not hold up his head, as it were, and strut in
his gait?

Sim. Yes, indeed, does he.

Quick. Well, Heaven send Anne Page no worse for-   30
tune! Tell Master Parson Evans I will do what I can
for your master. Anne is a good girl, and I wish—

[*Enter Rugby.*]

Rug. Out, alas! here comes my master.

34. **shent:** scolded.

35. **closet:** chamber.

38. **doubt;** fear.

42. **intend:** attend; hear.

46. **horn-mad:** enraged like a horned beast in the rutting season.

47–8. **ma foi, il fait fort chaud. Je m'en vais à la cour—la grande affaire:** on my word, it is very hot. I am going to court—great business.

50. **Oui, mette le au mon pocket:** yes, put it in my pocket.

58. **trot:** troth; faith; **Od's me:** God save me.

58–9. **Qu'ai-j'oublié:** what have I forgotten.

59. **simples:** herbs.

Quick. We shall all be shent. Run in here, good
young man: go into this closet. He will not stay long.   35
[*Shuts Simple in the closet.*] What, John Rugby! John!
what, John, I say! Go, John, go inquire for my master.
I doubt he be not well, that he comes not home.
    [*Singing*] And down, down, adown-a, etc.

[*Enter Doctor Caius.*]

Caius. Vat is you sing? I do not like des toys. Pray   40
you, go and vetch me in my closet *un boitier vert*, a
box, a green-a box. Do intend vat I speak? A green-a
box.

Quick. Ay, forsooth, I'll fetch it you. [*Aside*] I am
glad he went not in himself: if he had found the   45
young man, he would have been horn-mad.

Caius. Fe, fe, fe, fe! *ma foi, il fait fort chaud. Je
m'en vais à la cour—la grande affaire.*

Quick. Is it this, sir?

Caius. Oui, mette le au mon pocket: *dépêche,*   50
quickly. Vere is dat knave Rugby?

Quick. What, John Rugby! John!

Rug. Here, Sir!

Caius. You are John Rugby, and you are Jack Rugby. Come, take-a your rapier and come after my heel   55
to the court.

Rug. 'Tis ready, sir, here in the porch.

Caius. By my trot, I tarry too long. Od's me! *Qu'ai-
j'oublié?* Dere is some simples in my closet dat I vill
not for the varld I shall leave behind.   60

63. **diable:** devil.

63–4. **Vilenie, larron:** villain, thief.

70. **phlegmatic:** Quickly's mistake for "choleric" (angry).

71. **of:** on.

80–1. **put my finger in the fire:** i.e., prove her veracity with the ordeal by fire.

82. **baille:** bring.

86. **melancholy:** irascible.

Quick. Ay me, he'll find the young man there and
be mad!

Caius. O *diable, diable!* vat is in my closet? *Vilenie,
larron!* [*Pulling Simple out.*] Rugby, my rapier!

Quick. Good master, be content.   65

Caius. Wherefore shall I be content-a?

Quick. The young man is an honest man.

Caius. What shall de honest man do in my closet?
Dere is no honest man dat shall come in my closet.

Quick. I beseech you, be not so phlegmatic. Hear   70
the truth of it. He came of an errand to me from Parson Hugh.

Caius. Vell.

Sim. Ay, forsooth; to desire her to—

Quick. Peace, I pray you.   75

Caius. Peace-a your tongue. Speak-a your tale.

Sim. To desire this honest gentlewoman, your maid,
to speak a good word to Mistress Anne Page for my
master in the way of marriage.

Quick. This is all, indeed, la! but I'll ne'er put my 80
finger in the fire, and need not.

Caius. Sir Hugh send-a you? Rugby, *baille* me some
paper. Tarry you a little-a while.   [*Writes.*]

Quick. [*Aside to Simple*] I am glad he is so quiet:
if he had been thoroughly moved, you should have   85
heard him so loud and so melancholy. But notwithstanding, man, I'll do you your master what good I
can: and the very yea and the no is, the French doctor, my master—I may call him my master, look you,
for I keep his house; and I wash, wring, brew, bake, 90

93. **charge:** burden.

95. **Are you avised o' that:** do you realize that.

111. **Jack:** rascal.

112. **measure our weapon:** referee the duel.

115–16. **goodyear:** the exact meaning and derivation of the word are uncertain, but it is used in a similar way to "plague" or "devil" in exclamations such as this.

scour, dress meat and drink, make the beds, and do
all myself—

Sim. [*Aside to Quickly*] 'Tis a great charge to come
under one body's hand.

Quick. [*Aside to Simple*] Are you avised o' that? 95
You shall find it a great charge; and to be up early
and down late. But notwithstanding—to tell you in
your ear; I would have no words of it—my master
himself is in love with Mistress Anne Page: but notwithstanding that I know Anne's mind, that's neither 100
here nor there.

Caius. You jack'nape, give-a this letter to Sir Hugh.
By gar, it is a shallenge! I will cut his troat in de park;
and I will teach a scurvy jackanape priest to meddle
or make.—You may be gone: it is not good you tarry 105
here.—By gar, I will cut all his two stones. By gar, he
shall not have a stone to throw at his dog.

[*Exit Simple.*]

Quick. Alas, he speaks but for his friend.

Caius. It is no matter-a ver dat. Do not you tell-a
me dat I shall have Anne Page for myself? By gar, I 110
vill kill de Jack priest; and I have appointed mine
host of de Jarteer to measure our weapon. By gar, I
will myself have Anne Page.

Quick. Sir, the maid loves you, and all shall be well.
We must give folks leave to prate. What, the good- 115
year!

Caius. Rugby, come to the court with me. By gar,
if I have not Anne Page, I shall turn your head out of

120. **An:** pun on Anne.

125. **trow:** wonder; **near:** into.

131. **honest:** chaste.

134. **do any good:** have any luck.

141–42. **it is such another Nan:** i.e., Anne is such a lively girl; **detest:** protest.

my door. Follow my heels, Rugby.

> [*Exeunt Caius and Rugby.*]

Quick. You shall have An fool's-head of your own. 120
No, I know Anne's mind for that: never a woman in
Windsor knows more of Anne's mind than I do; nor
can do more than I do with her, I thank Heaven.

Fen. [*Within*] Who's within there? ho!

Quick. Who's there, I trow? Come near the house, 125
I pray you.

[*Enter Fenton.*]

Fen. How now, good woman! How dost thou?

Quick. The better that it pleases your good Worship to ask.

Fen. What news? How does pretty Mistress Anne? 130

Quick. In truth, sir, and she is pretty, and honest,
and gentle; and one that is your friend, I can tell you
that by the way, I praise Heaven for it.

Fen. Shall I do any good, thinkst thou? Shall I not
lose my suit? 135

Quick. Troth, sir, all is in His hands above: but notwithstanding, Master Fenton, I'll be sworn on a book,
she loves you. Have not your Worship a wart above
your eye?

Fen. Yes, marry, have I. What of that? 140

Quick. Well, thereby hangs a tale. Good faith, it is
such another Nan! but, I detest, an honest maid as
ever broke bread. We had an hour's talk of that wart.
I shall never laugh but in that maid's company! But,

145. **allicholy:** melancholy.
146. **go to:** I've said enough.
149. **commend me:** give her my respects.
152. **confidence:** conference; conversation.

indeed, she is given too much to allicholy and mus-   145
ing: but for you—well, go to.

Fen. Well, I shall see her today. Hold, there's
money for thee: let me have thy voice in my behalf.
If thou seest her before me, commend me.

Quick. Will I? I' faith, that we will; and I will tell   150
your Worship more of the wart the next time we have
confidence; and of other wooers.

Fen. Well, farewell. I am in great haste now.

Quick. Farewell to your Worship. [*Exit Fenton.*]
Truly, an honest gentleman: but Anne loves him not;   155
for I know Anne's mind as well as another does. Out
upon't! what have I forgot?

                                        Exit.

THE
MERRY WIVES
OF
WINDSOR

ACT II

II.i. Mrs. Page is astonished at receiving a love letter from Falstaff. Her friend Mrs. Ford comes to visit and reveals that she too has had a love letter from the fat knight. Both women are outraged that Falstaff should so misunderstand their characters and decide to teach him a lesson by leading him on and ultimately making a fool of him. In the meantime, Pistol and Nym have come to warn Ford and Page of Falstaff's attempt on the honor of their wives. When Mrs. Quickly arrives to see Anne Page, the two women ask her to deliver messages to Falstaff. Shallow and the host of the Garter appear and report that Sir Hugh Evans and Dr. Caius are to fight a duel. Ford privately asks the host to arrange for him to be introduced to Falstaff as a Mr. Brook. Unlike Page, he is not certain of his wife's loyalty and has determined to put it to the test.

iiiiiiiiiiiiiiiiiiiiiiiiiiiiiiii

4–6. though Love use Reason for his precisian, he admits him not for his counselor: i.e., although the lover may listen to the preachings of Reason, he will not be ruled by his advice. Cf. the proverb "Love is without reason."

8. sack: sherry wine.

20. Herod of Jewry: as a character in biblical plays, Herod usually spoke in an inflated style that was comic in effect.

ACT II

Scene I. [Before Page's house.]

Enter Mistress Page, [with a letter].

Mrs. Page. What, have I scaped love letters in the
holiday time of my beauty, and am I now a subject
for them? Let me see.   [*Reads.*]
"Ask me no reason why I love you, for though
Love use Reason for his precisian, he admits him not   5
for his counselor. You are not young, no more am I:
go to, then, there's sympathy. You are merry, so am
I: ha, ha! then there's more sympathy. You love sack,
and so do I: would you desire better sympathy? Let
it suffice thee, Mistress Page, at the least, if the love   10
of soldier can suffice, that I love thee. I will not say
pity me, 'tis not a soldier-like phrase; but I say, love
me. By me,

> Thine own true knight,
> By day or night,   15
> Or any kind of light,
> With all his might
> For thee to fight,
>
> JOHN FALSTAFF."

What a Herod of Jewry is this! O wicked, wicked   20

23

22. **unweighed:** i.e., weightless; light.

23. **Flemish drunkard:** Falstaff is only **Flemish** in being a **drunkard.** Englishmen attributed drunkenness as a national characteristic to Dutchmen, Danes, and Germans.

24. **conversation:** behavior.

28. **exhibit:** put forward.

36–7. **to show:** i.e., something to show.

world! One that is well-nigh worn to pieces with age
to show himself a young gallant! What an unweighed
behavior hath this Flemish drunkard picked—with
the Devil's name!—out of my conversation, that he
dares in this manner assay me? Why, he hath not   25
been thrice in my company! What should I say to
him? I was then frugal of my mirth. Heaven forgive
me! Why, I'll exhibit a bill in the parliament for the
putting down of men. How shall I be revenged on
him? for revenged I will be, as sure as his guts are   30
made of puddings.

[*Enter Mistress Ford.*]

Mrs. Ford. Mistress Page! trust me, I was going to
your house.

Mrs. Page. And, trust me, I was coming to you. You
look very ill.   35

Mrs. Ford. Nay, I'll ne'er believe that: I have to
show to the contrary.

Mrs. Page. Faith, but you do, in my mind.

Mrs. Ford. Well, I do, then; yet, I say, I could
show you to the contrary. O Mistress Page, give me   40
some counsel!

Mrs. Page. What's the matter, woman?

Mrs. Ford. O woman, if it were not for one trifling
respect, I could come to such honor!

Mrs. Page. Hang the trifle, woman! take the honor.   45
What is it? Dispense with trifles; what is it?

49–51. **These knights will hack; and so thou shouldst not alter the article of thy gentry:** knights are no longer in as high repute as they were; so you should not change your rank. **Hack** also has a sexual connotation and **gentry** puns on the word "gender."

52. **burn daylight:** waste time.

54–5. **make difference of men's liking:** differentiate between men's appearances.

57. **uncomeliness:** impropriety.

59. **gone:** conformed.

76. **press:** (1) printing press; (2) his embrace.

Mrs. Ford. If I would but go to hell for an eternal
moment or so, I could be knighted.

Mrs. Page. What? Thou liest! Sir Alice Ford! These
knights will hack; and so thou shouldst not alter the   50
article of thy gentry.

Mrs. Ford. We burn daylight. Here, read, read: perceive how I might be knighted. I shall think the
worse of fat men, as long as I have an eye to make
difference of men's liking: and yet he would not   55
swear, praised women's modesty, and gave such or-
derly and well-behaved reproof to all uncomeliness
that I would have sworn his disposition would have
gone to the truth of his words; but they do no more
adhere and keep place together than the Hundredth   60
Psalm to the tune of "Greensleeves." What tempest,
I trow, threw this whale, with so many tuns of oil in
his belly, ashore at Windsor? How shall I be revenged on him? I think the best way were to entertain him with hope till the wicked fire of lust have   65
melted him in his own grease. Did you ever hear the
like?

Mrs. Page. Letter for letter, but that the name of
Page and Ford differs! To thy great comfort in this
mystery of ill opinions, here's the twin brother of thy   70
letter: but let thine inherit first, for, I protest, mine
never shall. I warrant he hath a thousand of these
letters, writ with blank space for different names—
sure, more—and these are of the second edition. He
will print them, out of doubt; for he cares not what   75
he puts into the press, when he would put us two. I

77. lie under Mount Pelion: a reference to the giants' placing of Pelion on Ossa in their effort to reach Olympus during their war with the gods.

78. lascivious turtles: turtledoves are proverbial models of faithful love.

83. wrangle with mine own honesty: call my own chastity in question.

83–4. entertain: receive; i.e., she doubts her own self-knowledge.

86. boarded: accosted.

93. fine-baited: offering false hope of success.

97–8. chariness of our honesty: prudent care of our chastity.

106. greasy: lustful.

Piling Pelion on Ossa.
From Gabrieli Simeoni, *La vita et Metamorfoseo d'Ovidio* (1559).

had rather be a giantess and lie under Mount Pelion.
Well, I will find you twenty lascivious turtles ere one
chaste man.

Mrs. Ford. Why, this is the very same; the very 80
hand, the very words. What doth he think of us?

Mrs. Page. Nay, I know not: it makes me almost
ready to wrangle with mine own honesty. I'll entertain myself like one that I am not acquainted withal;
for, sure, unless he know some strain in me that I 85
know not myself, he would never have boarded me
in this fury.

Mrs. Ford. "Boarding," call you it? I'll be sure to
keep him above deck.

Mrs. Page. So will I: if he come under my hatches, 90
I'll never to sea again. Let's be revenged on him: let's
appoint him a meeting, give him a show of comfort
in his suit, and lead him on with a fine-baited delay
till he hath pawned his horses to mine host of the
Garter. 95

Mrs. Ford. Nay, I will consent to act any villainy
against him that may not sully the chariness of our
honesty. O, that my husband saw this letter! It would
give eternal food to his jealousy.

Mrs. Page. Why, look where he comes, and my 100
goodman too. He's as far from jealousy as I am from
giving him cause; and that, I hope, is an unmeasur-
able distance.

Mrs. Ford. You are the happier woman.

Mrs. Page. Let's consult together against this 105
greasy knight. Come hither.   [*They retire.*]

108. **curtal:** docktailed; i.e., in this context, "useless."

114. **gallimaufry:** in cookery, a mixture of many ingredients; i.e., a variety; **perpend:** think it over.

116. **liver:** considered the seat of love.

117. **Actaeon:** a hunter in mythology who saw Diana bathing and was changed to a stag, which his own hounds devoured. Because of the stag's horns, he was also associated with the horned cuckold (betrayed husband). **Ringwood** was a typical name for a hound.

123–24. **cuckoo birds do sing:** the note of the cuckoo (which sounds much like "cuckold") would be irksome to a man who suspected his wife's fidelity.

130. **humored:** Nym's speech satirizes the affected tags that were popular in this period. The word "humor" is constantly used by him in a meaningless manner.

Actaeon and his hounds.
From Henry Peacham, *Minerva Britanna* (1612).

[*Enter Ford, with Pistol, and Page, with Nym.*]

Ford. Well, I hope it be not so.
Pis. Hope is a curtal-dog in some affairs.
Sir John affects thy wife.
  Ford. Why, sir, my wife is not young.   110
  Pis. He woos both high and low, both rich and
    poor,
Both young and old, one with another, Ford.
He loves the gallimaufry. Ford, perpend.
  Ford. Love my wife!   115
  Pis. With liver burning hot. Prevent, or go thou,
Like Sir Actaeon be, with Ringwood at thy heels.
O, odious is the name!
  Ford. What name, sir?
  Pis. The horn, I say. Farewell.   120
Take heed; have open eye; for thieves do foot by
    night.
Take heed, ere summer comes, or cuckoo birds do
    sing.
Away, Sir Corporal Nym!—   125
Believe it, Page: he speaks sense.   [*Exit.*]
  Ford. [*Aside*] I will be patient; I will find out this.
  Nym. [*To Page*] And this is true: I like not the hu-
mor of lying. He hath wronged me in some humors. I
should have borne the humored letter to her; but I 130
have a sword, and it shall bite upon my necessity.
He loves your wife: there's the short and the long.
My name is Corporal Nym: I speak and I avouch;

139. **his:** its.

144. **Cataian:** scoundrel. The Chinese (men of Cathay) had thus early acquired a reputation for sharp dealing.

146. **true:** honest.

154. **crotchets:** odd notions.

156. **Have with you:** let's be off.

'Tis true: my name is Nym, and Falstaff loves your
wife.   135
Adieu. I love not the humor of bread and cheese;
and there's the humor of it. Adieu.   [*Exit.*]

Page. [*Aside*] "The humor of it," quoth 'a! Here's a
fellow frights English out of his wits.

Ford. [*Aside*] I will seek out Falstaff.   140

Page. [*Aside*] I never heard such a drawling, affect-
ing rogue.

Ford. [*Aside*] If I do find it—well.

Page. [*Aside*] I will not believe such a Cataian,
though the priest o' the town commended him for a 145
true man.

Ford. [*Aside*] 'Twas a good sensible fellow—well.

[*Mrs. Page and Mrs. Ford come forward.*]

Page. How now, Meg!

Mrs. Page. Whither go you, George? Hark you.

Mrs. Ford. How now, sweet Frank! Why art thou 150
melancholy?

Ford. I melancholy! I am not melancholy. Get you
home, go.

Mrs. Ford. Faith, thou hast some crotchets in thy
head now. Will you go, Mistress Page?   155

Mrs. Page. Have with you. You'll come to dinner,
George? [*Aside to Mrs. Ford*] Look who comes yonder: she shall be our messenger to this paltry knight.

Mrs. Ford. [*Aside to Mrs. Page*] Trust me, I
thought on her: she'll fit it.   160

172. **offer:** dare.
173. **yoke:** pair.
174. **very:** unqualified.
185. **nothing:** i.e., no horns.

[Enter Mistress Quickly.]

Mrs. Page. You are come to see my daughter Anne?

Quick. Ay, forsooth; and, I pray, how does good Mistress Anne?

Mrs. Page. Go in with us and see: we have an hour's talk with you. 165

[Exeunt Mrs. Page, Mrs. Ford, and Mrs. Quickly.]

Page. How now, Master Ford!

Ford. You heard what this knave told me, did you not?

Page. Yes, and you heard what the other told me?

Ford. Do you think there is truth in them? 170

Page. Hang 'em, slaves! I do not think the knight would offer it: but these that accuse him in his intent towards our wives are a yoke of his discarded men; very rogues, now they be out of service.

Ford. Were they his men? 175

Page. Marry, were they.

Ford. I like it never the better for that. Does he lie at the Garter?

Page. Ay, marry, does he. If he should intend this voyage toward my wife, I would turn her loose to 180 him; and what he gets more of her than sharp words, let it lie on my head.

Ford. I do not misdoubt my wife; but I would be loath to turn them together. A man may be too confident: I would have nothing lie on my head. I cannot 185 be thus satisfied.

193–94. **and twenty:** and twenty more of them.
205. **contrary:** different.

Page. Look where my ranting host of the Garter
comes. There is either liquor in his pate, or money
in his purse, when he looks so merrily.

[*Enter Host.*]

How now, mine host!   190
    Host. How now, bullyrook! Thou'rt a gentleman.
Cavaleiro-justice, I say!

[*Enter Shallow.*]

Shal. I follow, mine host, I follow. Good even and
twenty, good Master Page! Master Page, will you go
with us? We have sport in hand.   195
    Host. Tell him, cavaleiro-justice. Tell him, bully-
rook.
    Shal. Sir, there is a fray to be fought between Sir
Hugh the Welsh priest and Caius the French doctor.
    Ford. Good mine host o' the Garter, a word with 200
you.   [*Drawing him aside.*]
    Host. What sayst thou, my bullyrook?
    Shal. [*To Page*] Will you go with us to behold it?
My merry host hath had the measuring of their weapons; and, I think, hath appointed them contrary 205
places; for, believe me, I hear the parson is no jester.
Hark, I will tell you what our sport shall be.
                           [*They converse apart.*]
    Host. Hast thou no suit against my knight, my
guest-cavaleire?

210. **pottle:** two-quart measure.

211. **burnt sack:** heated sherry.

215. **An-heires:** possibly a mistake for Dutch *mynheers* (masters).

220. **you stand on:** i.e., fencers in general make much of; **distance:** keeping proper distance between the combatants; **stoccadoes:** thrusts, from the French *escotade* or Italian *stoccata*. Continental fencing techniques were ousting the old English style.

222–23. **longsword:** now becoming an old-fashioned weapon.

223. **tall:** valiant.

228. **secure:** overconfident.

229. **frailty:** i.e., the frailty that is common to her sex. Ford means that he is foolish to trust his wife, who is as frail as her sex; he does not imply that she is peculiarly susceptible to temptation.

Longsword and buckler.
From Giacomo di Grassi, *True Art of Defense* (1594).

Ford. None, I protest: but I'll give you a pottle of   210
burnt sack to give me recourse to him, and tell him
my name is Brook—only for a jest.

Host. My hand, bully! Thou shalt have egress and
regress—said I well?—and thy name shall be Brook.
It is a merry knight. Will you go, An-heires?   215

Shal. Have with you, mine host.

Page. I have heard the Frenchman hath good skill
in his rapier.

Shal. Tut, sir, I could have told you more. In these
times you stand on distance, your passes, stoccadoes,   220
and I know not what. 'Tis the heart, Master Page: 'tis
here, 'tis here! I have seen the time with my longsword I would have made you four tall fellows skip
like rats.

Host. Here, boys, here, here! Shall we wag?   225

Page. Have with you. I had rather hear them scold
than fight.   [*Exeunt Host, Shallow, and Page.*]

Ford. Though Page be a secure fool, and stands so
firmly on his wife's frailty, yet I cannot put off my
opinion so easily. She was in his company at Page's   230
house; and what they made there I know not. Well,
I will look further into't: and I have a disguise to
sound Falstaff. If I find her honest, I lose not my
labor; if she be otherwise, 'tis labor well bestowed.
                                                  Exit.

II.ii. Quickly reports to Falstaff that Mrs. Ford expects her husband to be away from home between ten and eleven and he may visit her then. She also delivers an encouraging message from Mrs. Page and assures him falsely that neither woman knows of the other's love for him. Mrs. Page has suggested that he send Robin, his page, to act as a go-between for them. Falstaff is jubilant at this news and agrees to see Mr. Brook. Ford, disguised as Brook, tells Falstaff that he has long loved Mrs. Ford but has been unable to win her. He offers to finance Falstaff if he will seduce Mrs. Ford so that she can no longer claim chastity as an excuse for denying him. Falstaff boasts that he has already made an assignation with the woman and will report his success that evening. Ford departs in a rage of jealousy.

⁜⁜⁜⁜⁜⁜⁜⁜⁜⁜⁜⁜⁜⁜⁜⁜⁜⁜⁜

5. **lay my countenance to pawn:** use my patronage as surety to procure money.

5–6. **grated upon:** imposed upon.

8. **grate:** i.e., of prison; **geminy:** pair.

17–8. **A short knife and a throng:** i.e., go seek your living as a cutpurse.

18. **manor of Pickt-hatch:** a notorious tavern in Turnmill Street, London, frequented by rogues and harlots.

Scene II. [A room in the Garter Inn.]

Enter Falstaff and Pistol.

Fal. I will not lend thee a penny.

Pis. Why, then the world's mine oyster,
Which I with sword will open.

Fal. Not a penny. I have been content, sir, you
should lay my countenance to pawn: I have grated   5
upon my good friends for three reprieves for you and
your coach-fellow Nym; or else you had looked
through the grate, like a geminy of baboons. I am
damned in hell for swearing to gentlemen my friends
you were good soldiers and tall fellows; and when   10
Mistress Bridget lost the handle of her fan, I took't
upon mine honor thou hadst it not.

Pis. Didst not thou share? Hadst thou not fifteen-
pence?

Fal. Reason, you rogue, reason! Thinkst thou I'll en-   15
danger my soul gratis? At a word, hang no more
about me: I am no gibbet for you. Go. A short knife
and a throng! To your manor of Pickt-hatch! Go.
You'll not bear a letter for me, you rogue! You stand
upon your honor! Why, thou unconfinable baseness,   20
it is as much as I can do to keep the terms of my
honor precise. I, I, I myself sometimes, leaving the
fear of Heaven on the left hand and hiding mine
honor in my necessity, am fain to shuffle, to hedge,

25. **lurch:** lurk (with dishonest intent); **ensconce:** shelter.

26. **catamountain:** fierce; **red-lattice:** alehouse. Many alehouses were distinguished by red lattices at the windows.

34. **and't:** if it.

and to lurch; and yet you, rogue, will ensconce your   25
rags, your catamountain looks, your red-lattice
phrases, and your bold-beating oaths under the shelter of your honor! You will not do it, you!

Pis. I do relent. What would thou more of man?

[*Enter Robin.*]

Rob. Sir, here's a woman would speak with you.   30
Fal. Let her approach.

[*Enter Mistress Quickly.*]

Quick. Give your Worship good morrow.
Fal. Good morrow, goodwife.
Quick. Not so, and't please your Worship.
Fal. Good maid, then.   35
Quick. I'll be sworn;
As my mother was, the first hour I was born.
Fal. I do believe the swearer. What with me?
Quick. Shall I vouchsafe your Worship a word or
two?   40
Fal. Two thousand, fair woman: and I'll vouchsafe
thee the hearing.
Quick. There is one Mistress Ford, sir—I pray, come
a little nearer this ways. I myself dwell with Master
Doctor Caius—   45
Fal. Well, on: Mistress Ford, you say.
Quick. Your Worship says very true: I pray your
Worship, come a little nearer this ways.

59. **canaries:** a lively dance associated with the natives of the Canary Islands; this is Quickly's mistake for "quandary." The phrase to be "in a quandary" was already proverbial.

65. **rushling:** rustling.

73. **on:** of.

75. **pensioners:** Queen Elizabeth had a bodyguard known as the "Gentlemen Pensioners," composed of the tallest and handsomest of the youthful nobility.

78. **Mercury:** messenger.

Fal. I warrant thee, nobody hears: mine own people, mine own people.   50

Quick. Are they so? Heaven bless them, and make
them His servants!

Fal. Well, Mistress Ford: what of her?

Quick. Why, sir, she's a good creature.—Lord, Lord!
your Worship's a wanton! Well, Heaven forgive you   55
and all of us, I pray!

Fal. Mistress Ford: come, Mistress Ford.

Quick. Marry, this is the short and the long of it.
You have brought her into such a canaries as 'tis wonderful. The best courtier of them all, when the Court   60
lay at Windsor, could never have brought her to such
a canary. Yet there has been knights, and lords, and
gentlemen, with their coaches; I warrant you, coach
after coach, letter after letter, gift after gift; smelling
so sweetly, all musk, and so rushling, I warrant you,   65
in silk and gold; and in such alligant terms; and in
such wine and sugar of the best and the fairest, that
would have won any woman's heart; and, I warrant
you, they could never get an eye-wink of her. I had
myself twenty angels given me this morning; but I   70
defy all angels—in any such sort, as they say—but in
the way of honesty: and, I warrant you, they could
never get her so much as sip on a cup with the proud-
est of them all: and yet there has been earls, nay,
which is more, pensioners; but, I warrant you, all is   75
one with her.

Fal. But what says she to me? Be brief, my good
she-Mercury.

88. **frampold:** disagreeable.
95. **fartuous:** virtuous.

Quick. Marry, she hath received your letter; for the which she thanks you a thousand times; and she gives 80 you to notify that her husband will be absence from his house between ten and eleven.

Fal. Ten and eleven.

Quick. Ay, forsooth; and then you may come and see the picture, she says, that you wot of. Master 85 Ford, her husband, will be from home. Alas, the sweet woman leads an ill life with him! He's a very jealousy man. She leads a very frampold life with him, good heart.

Fal. Ten and eleven. Woman, commend me to her. 90 I will not fail her.

Quick. Why, you say well. But I have another messenger to your Worship. Mistress Page hath her hearty commendations to you, too: and let me tell you in your ear, she's as fartuous a civil modest wife, 95 and one, I tell you, that will not miss you morning nor evening prayer, as any is in Windsor, whoe'er be the other: and she bade me tell your Worship that her husband is seldom from home; but, she hopes there will come a time. I never knew a woman so 100 dote upon a man: surely, I think you have charms, la: yes, in truth.

Fal. Not I, I assure thee. Setting the attraction of my good parts aside, I have no other charms.

Quick. Blessing on your heart for't!   105

Fal. But, I pray thee, tell me this: has Ford's wife and Page's wife acquainted each other how they love me?

112. **of all loves:** if you love her.

112–13. **infection:** affection, inclination.

116. **list:** desires.

123. **nayword:** watchword.

132. **punk:** harlot.

133. **fights:** defensive screens on men-of-war.

135. **Sayst thou so:** is it true that you will accomplish this.

Quick. That were a jest indeed! They have not so
little grace, I hope: that were a trick indeed! But 110
Mistress Page would desire you to send her your little
page, of all loves. Her husband has a marvelous infection to the little page: and, truly, Master Page is an
honest man. Never a wife in Windsor leads a better
life than she does: do what she will, say what she will, 115
take all, pay all, go to bed when she list, rise when
she list, all is as she will. And, truly, she deserves it;
for if there be a kind woman in Windsor, she is one.
You must send her your page; no remedy.

Fal. Why, I will.   120

Quick. Nay, but do so, then: and, look you, he may
come and go between you both; and, in any case,
have a nayword, that you may know one another's
mind, and the boy never need to understand anything; for 'tis not good that children should know any 125
wickedness. Old folks, you know, have discretion, as
they say, and know the world.

Fal. Fare thee well. Commend me to them both.
There's my purse: I am yet thy debtor. Boy, go along
with this woman.   130

        [*Exeunt Mistress Quickly and Robin.*]
This news distracts me!

Pis. [*Aside*] This punk is one of Cupid's carriers:
Clap on more sails: pursue! up with your fights!
Give fire! She is my prize, or ocean whelm them all!
                                            [*Exit.*]

Fal. Sayst thou so, old Jack? Go thy ways: I'll make 135
more of thy old body than I have done. Will they yet

150. **encompassed:** achieved; **via:** let's go.
155–56. **Give us leave:** leave us.
156. **drawer:** tapster.

---

look after thee? Wilt thou, after the expense of so
much money, be now a gainer? Good body, I thank
thee. Let them say 'tis grossly done: so it be fairly
done, no matter.   140

[*Enter Bardolph.*]

Bar. Sir John, there's one Master Brook below
would fain speak with you and be acquainted with
you; and hath sent your Worship a morning's draught
of sack.

Fal. Brook is his name?   145

Bar. Ay, sir.

Fal. Call him in.   [*Exit Bardolph.*]
Such Brooks are welcome to me, that o'erflows such
liquor. Ah, ha! Mistress Ford and Mistress Page, have
I encompassed you? Go to: via!   150

[*Enter Bardolph, with Ford disguised as Brook.*]

Ford. Bless you, sir!

Fal. And you, sir! Would you speak with me?

Ford. I make bold to press with so little preparation
upon you.

Fal. You're welcome. What's your will? Give us   155
leave, drawer.   [*Exit Bardolph.*]

Ford. Sir, I am a gentleman that have spent much.
My name is Brook.

Fal. Good Master Brook, I desire more acquaintance of you.   160

164. **unseasoned:** unseasonable; inopportune.
170. **carriage:** burden.
185. **sith:** since.

An emblem expressing the thought of lines 204–5.
From Geoffrey Whitney, *A Choice of Emblems* (1586).

Ford. Good Sir John, I sue for yours: not to charge
you, for I must let you understand I think myself in
better plight for a lender than you are; the which hath
something emboldened me to this unseasoned intru-
sion: for they say, if money go before, all ways do lie 165
open.

Fal. Money is a good soldier, sir, and will on.

Ford. Troth, and I have a bag of money here troub-
les me. If you will help to bear it, Sir John, take all, or
half, for easing me of the carriage. 170

Fal. Sir, I know not how I may deserve to be your
porter.

Ford. I will tell you, sir, if you will give me the
hearing.

Fal. Speak, good Master Brook: I shall be glad to 175
be your servant.

Ford. Sir, I hear you are a scholar—I will be brief
with you—and you have been a man long known to
me, though I had never so good means as desire to
make myself acquainted with you. I shall discover a 180
thing to you wherein I must very much lay open mine
own imperfection: but, good Sir John, as you have
one eye upon my follies, as you hear them unfolded,
turn another into the register of your own, that I may
pass with a reproof the easier, sith you yourself know 185
how easy it is to be such an offender.

Fal. Very well, sir; proceed.

Ford. There is a gentlewoman in this town: her
husband's name is Ford.

Fal. Well, sir. 190

193. **observance:** attention; **engrossed:** hoarded.

193–94. **fee'd every slight occasion:** took every opportunity at all costs.

200. **meed:** reward.

220. **enlargeth her mirth so far:** is so merry.

Ford. I have long loved her, and, I protest to you,
bestowed much on her, followed her with a doting
observance, engrossed opportunities to meet her, fee'd
every slight occasion that could but niggardly give me
sight of her; not only bought many presents to give   195
her, but have given largely to many to know what
she would have given. Briefly, I have pursued her as
love hath pursued me, which hath been on the wing
of all occasions. But whatsoever I have merited, either
in my mind or in my means, meed, I am sure, I have   200
received none; unless experience be a jewel that I
have purchased at an infinite rate, and that hath
taught me to say this:

"Love like a shadow flies, when substance love
        pursues,   205
Pursuing that that flies, and flying what pursues."

Fal. Have you received no promise of satisfaction
at her hands?

Ford. Never.

Fal. Have you importuned her to such a purpose?   210

Ford. Never.

Fal. Of what quality was your love, then?

Ford. Like a fair house built on another man's
ground; so that I have lost my edifice by mistaking
the place where I erected it.   215

Fal. To what purpose have you unfolded this to
me?

Ford. When I have told you that, I have told you
all. Some say that though she appear honest to me, yet
in other places she enlargeth her mirth so far that   220

221. **shrewd construction:** malicious judgment.
224. **of great admittance:** i.e., welcome in the best circles; **authentic:** deservedly honored or recognized.
225. **allowed:** given credit.
226. **preparations:** accomplishments.
231. **amiable:** loving; amorous.
239. **folly:** lewdness.
241. **against:** directly at.
244. **ward:** shelter; defense.

there is shrewd construction made of her. Now, Sir
John, here is the heart of my purpose: you are a
gentleman of excellent breeding, admirable discourse,
of great admittance, authentic in your place and
person, generally allowed for your many warlike,   225
courtlike, and learned preparations.

Fal. O, sir!

Ford. Believe it, for you know it. There is money:
spend it, spend it; spend more; spend all I have! Only
give me so much of your time in exchange of it as to   230
lay an amiable siege to the honesty of this Ford's
wife. Use your art of wooing: win her to consent to
you. If any man may, you may as soon as any.

Fal. Would it apply well to the vehemency of your
affection that I should win what you would enjoy?   235
Methinks you prescribe to yourself very preposter-
ously.

Ford. O, understand my drift. She dwells so
securely on the excellency of her honor that the folly
of my soul dares not present itself: she is too bright   240
to be looked against. Now, could I come to her with
any detection in my hand, my desires had instance
and argument to commend themselves. I could drive
her then from the ward of her purity, her reputation,
her marriage vow, and a thousand other her defenses,   245
which now are too too strongly embattled against me.
What say you to't, Sir John?

Fal. Master Brook, I will first make bold with your
money; next, give me your hand; and last, as I am a
gentleman, you shall, if you will, enjoy Ford's wife.   250

253. **Want:** lack.

262. **speed:** prosper.

267. **wittolly:** a "wittol" is a man who tolerates his wife's infidelity. Falstaff means that Ford is too stupid or weak to notice Mrs. Ford's misbehavior.

270. **there's my harvest home:** that's where I'll reap my profit.

273. **mechanical:** a contemptuous adjective for a manual laborer; base; **salt-butter:** rank-smelling.

276–77. **predominate:** rule (used in an astrological sense).

279. **aggravate his style:** supplement his title (with that of "cuckold").

Ford. O good sir!

Fal. I say you shall.

Ford. Want no money, Sir John: you shall want
none.

Fal. Want no Mistress Ford, Master Brook: you   255
shall want none. I shall be with her, I may tell you, by
her own appointment. Even as you came in to me,
her assistant, or go-between, parted from me. I say I
shall be with her between ten and eleven, for at that
time the jealous, rascally knave her husband will be   260
forth. Come you to me at night: you shall know how I
speed.

Ford. I am blest in your acquaintance. Do you
know Ford, sir?

Fal. Hang him, poor cuckoldly knave! I know him   265
not: yet I wrong him to call him poor. They say the
jealous wittolly knave hath masses of money, for the
which his wife seems to me well favored. I will use
her as the key of the cuckoldly rogue's coffer; and
there's my harvest home.   270

Ford. I would you knew Ford, sir, that you might
avoid him, if you saw him.

Fal. Hang him, mechanical salt-butter rogue! I will
stare him out of his wits. I will awe him with my
cudgel: it shall hang like a meteor o'er the cuckold's   275
horns. Master Brook, thou shalt know I will predominate over the peasant, and thou shalt lie with
his wife. Come to me soon at night. Ford's a knave,
and I will aggravate his style. Thou, Master Brook,

281. **soon at night:** tonight.

284. **improvident:** reckless; lacking foundation.

289–90. **stand under the adoption of:** be forced to accept; **terms:** epithets.

293. **additions:** names.

A cuckold and his wife.
From a seventeenth-century ballad.

shalt know him for knave and cuckold. Come to me   280
soon at night.   [*Exit.*]

Ford. What a damned Epicurean rascal is this!
My heart is ready to crack with impatience. Who says
this is improvident jealousy? My wife hath sent to
him; the hour is fixed; the match is made. Would any   285
man have thought this? See the hell of having a false
woman! My bed shall be abused, my coffers ran-
sacked, my reputation gnawn at; and I shall not only
receive this villainous wrong, but stand under the
adoption of abominable terms, and by him that does   290
me this wrong. Terms! names!—Amaimon sounds well;
Lucifer, well; Barbason, well; yet they are devils'
additions, the names of fiends: but Cuckold! Wittol!
—Cuckold! the Devil himself hath not such a name.
Page is an ass, a secure ass: he will trust his wife; he   295
will not be jealous. I will rather trust a Fleming with
my butter, Parson Hugh the Welshman with my
cheese, an Irishman with my aqua vitae bottle, or a
thief to walk my ambling gelding than my wife with
herself. Then she plots, then she ruminates, then she   300
devises; and what they think in their hearts they may
effect, they will break their hearts but they will
effect. Heaven be praised for my jealousy! Eleven
o'clock the hour. I will prevent this, detect my wife,
be revenged on Falstaff, and laugh at Page. I will   305
about it: better three hours too soon than a minute
too late. Fie, fie, fie! cuckold! cuckold! cuckold!

                                              Exit.

II.iii. Caius and his man Rugby seek Sir Hugh at the supposed place of meeting. The latter has not arrived, and when the host, Shallow, Slender, and Page come to see the fun, the host persuades Caius to go with him to Frogmore, where he will find Anne Page. He covertly sends the other to find Evans, who is also at Frogmore, in order to bring the two together.

▪▪▪▪▪▪▪▪▪▪▪▪▪▪▪▪▪▪▪▪▪▪▪▪▪▪▪▪

11. **de herring is no dead so as:** i.e., no herring is so dead as.

Scene III. [A field near Windsor.]

Enter Caius and Rugby.

Caius. Jack Rugby!

Rug. Sir?

Caius. Vat is the clock, Jack?

Rug. 'Tis past the hour, sir, that Sir Hugh promised
to meet.   5

Caius. By gar, he has save his soul dat he is no
come. He has pray his Pible well dat he is no come.
By gar, Jack Rugby, he is dead already if he be come.

Rug. He is wise, sir: he knew your Worship would
kill him if he came.   10

Caius. By gar, de herring is no dead so as I vill kill
him. Take your rapier, Jack: I vill tell you how I vill
kill him.

Rug. Alas, sir, I cannot fence.

Caius. Villainy, take your rapier.   15

Rug. Forbear. Here's company.

[*Enter Host, Shallow, Slender, and Page.*]

Host. Bless thee, bully doctor!

Shal. Save you, Master Doctor Caius!

Page. Now, good Master Doctor!

Slen. Give you good morrow, sir.   20

Caius. Vat be all you, one, two, tree, four, come for?

22. **foin:** thrust.

23. **traverse:** move from side to side.

24. **pass thy punto:** employ thy point; **stock:** stoccado; see II.i.220; **reverse:** backhanded thrust.

25. **montant:** upright thrust.

26. **Francisco:** Frenchman; **Aesculapius:** in classical mythology, the god of medicine and healing.

27. **Galen:** Greek physician (A.D. 130–200) and writer on medicine; **heart of elder:** heart of soft pulp; coward.

27–8. **bully-stale:** my fine assayer of horse urine. Contemporary medicine relied heavily on urinalysis for diagnosis.

31. **Castalion-King-Urinal:** pun on "Castilian King" and "cast stallion," with further reference to urinalysis.

31–2. **Hector of Greece:** mock praise of his fighting prowess. Hector, of course, was a Trojan, not a Greek hero.

37. **against the hair of:** contrary to the spirit of.

41. **Bodykins:** God's little body.

42. **of the peace:** i.e., a justice of the peace.

43. **make one:** join in.

Host. To see thee fight, to see thee foin, to see thee
traverse; to see thee here, to see thee there; to see thee
pass thy punto, thy stock, thy reverse, thy distance,
thy montant. Is he dead, my Ethiopian? Is he dead,   25
my Francisco? Ha, bully! What says my Aesculapius?
my Galen? my heart of elder? Ha! is he dead, bully-
stale? is he dead?

Caius. By gar, he is de coward Jack priest of de
vorld: he is not show his face.   30

Host. Thou art a Castalion-King-Urinal. Hector of
Greece, my boy!

Caius. I pray you, bear vitness that me have stay six
or seven, two, tree hours for him, and he is no come.

Shal. He is the wiser man, Master Doctor: he is a   35
curer of souls, and you a curer of bodies. If you
should fight, you go against the hair of your profes-
sions. Is it not true, Master Page?

Page. Master Shallow, you have yourself been a
great fighter, though now a man of peace.   40

Shal. Bodykins, Master Page, though I now be old
and of the peace, if I see a sword out, my finger itches
to make one. Though we are justices and doctors and
churchmen, Master Page, we have some salt of our
youth in us: we are the sons of women, Master Page.   45

Page. 'Tis true, Master Shallow.

Shal. It will be found so, Master Page. Master
Doctor Caius, I am come to fetch you home. I am
sworn of the peace: you have showed yourself a wise
physician, and Sir Hugh hath shown himself a wise   50

54. **Mockwater:** another sneer at casting of urine.
61. **clapperclaw:** thrash; **tightly:** vigorously.
63. **make thee amends:** give thee thy deserts.
66. **wag:** be on his way.

and patient churchman. You must go with me, Master
Doctor.

Host. Pardon, guest-justice. A word, Mounseur
Mockwater.

Caius. Mockvater! vat is dat?   55

Host. Mockwater, in our English tongue, is valor,
bully.

Caius. By gar, then, I have as much mockvater as
de Englishman. Scurvy jack-dog priest! By gar, me
vill cut his ears.   60

Host. He will clapperclaw thee tightly, bully.

Caius. Clapper-de-claw! Vat is dat?

Host. That is, he will make thee amends.

Caius. By gar, me do look he shall clapper-de-claw
me; for, by gar, me vill have it.   65

Host. And I will provoke him to't, or let him wag.

Caius. Me tank you for dat.

Host. And, moreover, bully—[*Aside to them.*] But
first, Master guest, and Master Page, and eke Cava-
leiro Slender, go you through the town to Frogmore. 70

Page. Sir Hugh is there, is he?

Host. He is there. See what humor he is in; and I
will bring the doctor about by the fields. Will it do
well?

Shal. We will do it.   75

Page, Shal., Slen. Adieu, good Master Doctor.
              [*Exeunt Page, Shallow, and Slender.*]

Caius. By gar, me vill kill de priest, for he speak for
a jackanape to Anne Page.

Host. Let him die: sheathe thy impatience; throw

83. **Cried game:** your game is descried; there's your sport.

cold water on thy choler. Go about the fields with me   80
through Frogmore. I will bring thee where Mistress
Anne Page is, at a farmhouse a-feasting, and thou
shalt woo her. Cried game! Said I well?

Caius. By gar, me dank you vor dat. By gar, I love
you; and I shall procure-a you de good guest, de earl,   85
de knight, de lords, de gentlemen, my patients.

Host. For the which I will be thy adversary toward
Anne Page. Said I well?

Caius. By gar, 'tis good: vell said.

Host. Let us wag, then.   90

Caius. Come at my heels, Jack Rugby.

Exeunt.

THE
MERRY WIVES
OF
WINDSOR

ACT III

III.i. Evans has been awaiting the French doctor at Frogmore and questions Simple, who reports that he has sought in vain in all directions but toward the town. The others bring Caius and steer the pair into verbal instead of physical combat. Caius and Evans finally perceive that they are being made fools of and agree to get even with the host.

━━━━━━━━━━━━━━

5. **the petty-ward:** toward Windsor Little Park; **the park-ward:** toward Windsor Great Park.

6. **Old Windsor way:** toward Old Windsor, as compared with the newer part of the town.

14. **costard:** head (from the apple of the same name).

16. **To shallow . . . etc.:** from Marlowe's poem "Come Live with Me and Be My Love"; **falls:** cadences.

ACT III

Scene I. [A field near Frogmore.]

Enter Evans and Simple.

Evans. I pray you now, good Master Slender's serv-
ingman, and friend Simple by your name, which way
have you looked for Master Caius, that calls himself
doctor of physic?

Sim. Marry, sir, the petty-ward, the park-ward, 5
every way; Old Windsor way, and every way but the
town way.

Evans. I most fehemently desire you you will also
look that way.

Sim. I will, sir. 10

Evans. Pless my soul, how full of chollors I am, and
trempling of mind! I shall be glad if he have deceived
me. How melancholies I am! I will knog his urinals
about his knave's costard when I have good opportunities for the ork. Pless my soul! 15

[*Sings.*]

To shallow rivers, to whose falls
Melodious birds sings madrigals;

47

23. **Whenas I sat in Pabylon:** a line interpolated
from Psalm 137.

24. **vagram:** fragrant.

There will we make our peds of roses,
And a thousand fragrant posies.
          To shallow—   20
Mercy on me! I have a great dispositions to cry.

                                        [*Sings.*]

Melodious birds sing madrigals—
Whenas I sat in Pabylon—
And a thousand vagram posies.
          To shallow, etc.   25

Sim. Yonder he is, coming this way, Sir Hugh.
Evans. He's welcome.

                                        [*Sings.*]

          To shallow rivers, to whose falls—
Heaven prosper the right! What weapons is he?

Sim. No weapons, sir. There comes my master,   30
Master Shallow, and another gentleman, from Frogmore, over the stile, this way.

Evans. Pray you, give me my gown, or else keep it
in your arms.

[*Enter Page, Shallow, and Slender.*]

Shal. How now, Master Parson! Good morrow, good   35
Sir Hugh. Keep a gamester from the dice, and a good
student from his book, and it is wonderful.

Slen. [*Aside*] Ah, sweet Anne Page!

Page. Save you, good Sir Hugh!

Evans. Pless you from His mercy sake, all of you!   40

43. **doublet and hose:** close-fitting jacket, breeches, and stockings. Evans has presumably doffed his gown, normally worn by men of his profession, to have greater freedom of movement for his duel.

49. **reverend:** dignified.

50. **belike:** perhaps.

50–51. **is at most odds with his own gravity:** i.e., behaves in a manner more unbecoming his dignity.

55. **so wide of his own respect:** so forgetful of the dignity of such a man as himself.

Shal. What, the sword and the Word! Do you study them both, Master Parson?

Page. And youthful still! In your doublet and hose this raw rheumatic day?

Evans. There is reasons and causes for it.   45

Page. We are come to you to do a good office, Master Parson.

Evans. Fery well: what is it?

Page. Yonder is a most reverend gentleman, who, belike having received wrong by some person, is at   50
most odds with his own gravity and patience that ever you saw.

Shal. I have lived fourscore years and upward: I never heard a man of his place, gravity, and learning so wide of his own respect.   55

Evans. What is he?

Page. I think you know him: Master Doctor Caius, the renowned French physician.

Evans. Got's will, and His passion of my heart! I had as lief you would tell me of a mess of porridge.   60

Page. Why?

Evans. He has no more knowledge in Hibocrates and Galen; and he is a knave besides, a cowardly knave as you would desires to be acquainted withal.

Page. I warrant you, he's the man should fight with   65
him.

Slen. [*Aside*] O sweet Anne Page!

Shal. It appears so, by his weapons. Keep them asunder: here comes Doctor Caius.

73. **question:** argue.
85. **cogscomb:** head.
93. **Gallia:** "Wallia," for Wales.

[*Enter Host, Caius, and Rugby.*]

Page. Nay, good Master Parson, keep in your   70
weapon.

Shal. So do you, good Master Doctor.

Host. Disarm them and let them question: let them
keep their limbs whole and hack our English.

Caius. I pray you, let-a me speak a word with your   75
ear. Verefore vill you not meet-a me?

Evans. [*Aside to Caius*] Pray you, use your patience: in good time.

Caius. By gar, you are de coward, de jack dog,
John ape.   80

Evans. [*Aside to Caius*] Pray you, let us not be
laughingstocks to other men's humors. I desire you in
friendship, and I will one way or other make you
amends. [*Aloud*] I will knog your urinals about your
knave's cogscomb for missing your meetings and ap-   85
pointments.

Caius. Diable! Jack Rugby, mine host de Jarteer,
have I not stay for him to kill him? Have I not, at de
place I did appoint?

Evans. As I am a Christians soul, now, look you,   90
this is the place appointed. I'll be judgment by mine
host of the Garter.

Host. Peace, I say, Gallia and Gaul, French and
Welsh, soul-curer and body-curer!

Caius. Ay, dat is very good: excellent.   95

Host. Peace, I say! hear mine host of the Garter.

100–101. **no-verbs:** i.e., faulty English.

105. **issue:** outcome.

111. **sot:** fool.

112–13. **vloutingstog:** laughingstock.

115. **scall:** scald, meaning the same as **scurvy** (scabrous, contemptible); **cogging:** deceiving; **companion:** fellow (contemptuous).

Am I politic? Am I subtle? Am I a Machiavel? Shall I
lose my doctor? No: he gives me the potions and the
motions. Shall I lose my parson, my priest, my Sir
Hugh? No: he gives me the proverbs and the no-   100
verbs. Give me thy hand, terrestrial: so! Give me thy
hand, celestial: so! Boys of art, I have deceived you
both: I have directed you to wrong places. Your hearts
are mighty, your skins are whole, and let burnt sack
be the issue. Come, lay their swords to pawn. Follow   105
me, lads of peace: follow, follow, follow!

Shal. Trust me, a mad host. Follow, gentlemen,
follow.

Slen. [*Aside*] O sweet Anne Page!

       [*Exeunt Shallow, Slender, Page, and Host.*]

Caius. Ha, do I perceive dat? Have you make-a de   110
sot of us, ha, ha?

Evans. This is well: he has made us his vloutingstog. I desire you that we may be friends; and let us
knog our prains together to be revenge on this same
scall, scurvy, cogging companion, the host of the   115
Garter.

Caius. By gar, with all my heart. He promise to
bring me where is Anne Page. By gar, he deceive me
too.

Evans. Well, I will smite his noddles. Pray you,   120
follow.

                              [*Exeunt.*]

III.ii. Ford meets Mrs. Page with Robin, on their way to see his wife. He feels certain that Page's wife is no more to be trusted than is his own. He expects to surprise Falstaff with his wife and to reveal Mrs. Page's wrongdoing to her husband. Page and the others appear and Ford invites them to his home, but Slender excuses himself because of a previous engagement to dine with Anne Page. Page has promised him her hand. The host speaks up for Fenton, but Page feels that Fenton has wasted his fortunes with Prince Hal and his riotous company and he has no intention of bettering Fenton's estate with his daughter's dowry. Ford persuades Caius, Page, and Evans to accompany him home, where he promises to reveal a monster. Shallow and Slender go off to keep their appointment with Anne Page, and the host returns to drink with Falstaff.

3. **Whether:** which.

Scene II. [A street in Windsor.]

Enter Mistress Page and Robin.

Mrs. Page. Nay, keep your way, little gallant: you
were wont to be a follower, but now you are a leader.
Whether had you rather, lead mine eyes, or eye your
master's heels?

Rob. I had rather, forsooth, go before you like a   5
man than follow him like a dwarf.

Mrs. Page. O, you are a flattering boy. Now I see
you'll be a courtier.

[*Enter Ford.*]

Ford. Well met, Mistress Page. Whither go you?

Mrs. Page. Truly, sir, to see your wife. Is she at   10
home?

Ford. Ay, and as idle as she may hang together, for
want of company. I think, if your husbands were
dead, you two would marry.

Mrs. Page. Be sure of that: two other husbands.   15

Ford. Where had you this pretty weathercock?

Mrs. Page. I cannot tell what the dickens his name
is my husband had him of. What do you call your
knight's name, sirrah?

Rob. Sir John Falstaff.   20

Ford. Sir John Falstaff!

30–1. **twelve score:** twelvescore yards.
31. **pieces out:** gives scope to.
32. **folly:** wantonness.
35. **revolted:** unfaithful.
37. **torture:** punish.
40–1. **cry aim:** offer encouragement (like spectators at an archery contest).

Mrs. Page. He, he: I can never hit on's name. There
is such a league between my goodman and he! Is your
wife at home indeed?

Ford. Indeed she is.   25

Mrs. Page. By your leave, sir: I am sick till I see her.
                              [*Exeunt Mrs. Page and Robin.*]

Ford. Has Page any brains? Hath he any eyes?
Hath he any thinking? Sure, they sleep: he hath no
use of them. Why, this boy will carry a letter twenty
mile, as easy as a cannon will shoot point-blank twelve   30
score. He pieces out his wife's inclination; he gives
her folly motion and advantage: and now she's going
to my wife, and Falstaff's boy with her. A man may
hear this show'r sing in the wind. And Falstaff's boy
with her! Good plots, they are laid, and our revolted   35
wives share damnation together. Well, I will take him,
then torture my wife, pluck the borrowed veil of
modesty from the so-seeming Mistress Page, divulge
Page himself for a secure and willful Actaeon; and to
these violent proceedings all my neighbors shall cry   40
aim. [*Clock heard.*] The clock gives me my cue, and
my assurance bids me search: there I shall find Falstaff. I shall be rather praised for this than mocked;
for it is as positive as the earth is firm that Falstaff is
there. I will go.   45

[*Enter Page, Shallow, Slender, Host, Sir Hugh Evans,
                    Caius, and Rugby.*]

47. **Trust me, a good knot:** on my word, a good company.

64. **holiday:** fine words.

65. **'Tis in his buttons:** his very buttons proclaim him a victor.

68. **having:** wealth.

69. **region:** station in life.

72. **simply:** i.e., without a dowry.

Shal., Page, etc. Well met, Master Ford.

Ford. Trust me, a good knot. I have good cheer at home, and I pray you all go with me.

Shal. I must excuse myself, Master Ford.

Slen. And so must I, sir. We have appointed to dine   50
with Mistress Anne, and I would not break with her for more money than I'll speak of.

Shal. We have lingered about a match between Anne Page and my cousin Slender, and this day we shall have our answer.   55

Slen. I hope I have your good will, father Page.

Page. You have, Master Slender: I stand wholly for you; but my wife, Master Doctor, is for you altogether.

Caius. Ay, be-gar; and de maid is love-a me. My   60
nursh-a Quickly tell me so mush.

Host. What say you to young Master Fenton? He capers, he dances, he has eyes of youth, he writes verses, he speaks holiday, he smells April and May. He will carry't, he will carry't. 'Tis in his buttons: he   65
will carry't.

Page. Not by my consent, I promise you. The gentleman is of no having: he kept company with the wild Prince and Poins. He is of too high a region; he knows too much. No, he shall not knit a knot in his   70
fortunes with the finger of my substance. If he take her, let him take her simply. The wealth I have waits on my consent, and my consent goes not that way.

76. **monster:** i.e., a cuckold.

83. **canary:** a sweet wine.

84. **pipe wine:** wine from a pipe (cask). This phrase must have a hidden meaning, now lost, since Ford has no real intention of drinking with Falstaff. A pun on paying the piper and the dance (canary) seems obvious.

85. **gentles:** gentlemen.

‖‖‖

III.iii. Mrs. Ford has arranged that Mrs. Page report the imminent arrival of Ford during Falstaff's visit, and her servants are alerted to remove a clothes basket at the appropriate moment. Falstaff has no more than paid Mrs. Ford compliments when Mrs. Page hurries in with her warning and Falstaff is hustled into the clothes basket. Ford questions the servants about the basket but accepts their explanation that they are taking the dirty laundry to be washed at Datchet Mead. Locking the door, Ford has his friends help him search, in vain. Page and the others reproach Ford for his unreasonable jealousy and he is temporarily mollified.

‖‖‖‖‖‖‖‖‖‖‖‖‖‖‖‖‖‖‖‖‖‖‖‖‖‖‖‖‖‖

2. **buck basket:** a container for dirty clothes.

Ford. I beseech you heartily, some of you go home
with me to dinner: besides your cheer, you shall have   75
sport. I will show you a monster. Master Doctor, you
shall go; so shall you, Master Page; and you, Sir
Hugh.

Shal. Well, fare you well: we shall have the freer
wooing at Master Page's.   80

                       [*Exeunt Shallow and Slender.*]

Caius. Go home, John Rugby: I come anon.

                       [*Exit Rugby.*]

Host. Farewell, my hearts. I will to my honest
knight Falstaff and drink canary with him.   [*Exit.*]

Ford. [*Aside*] I think I shall drink in pipe wine first
with him. I'll make him dance. Will you go, gentles?   85

All. Have with you, to see this monster.

                       Exeunt.

Scene III. [A room in Ford's house.]

Enter Mistress Ford and Mistress Page.

Mrs. Ford. What, John! What, Robert!
Mrs. Page. Quickly, quickly!—is the buck basket—
Mrs. Ford. I warrant. What, Robin, I say!

[*Enter Servants with a basket.*]

9. **hard:** near.

11. **staggering:** delay.

13. **whitsters:** bleachers; **Datchet Mead:** a meadow between Windsor Little Park and the Thames.

20. **eyas-musket:** unfledged, male sparrow hawk.

24. **Jack-a-Lent:** puppet. Literally, a straw doll used as a target in a Lenten game.

Mrs. Page. Come, come, come.

Mrs. Ford. Here, set it down.   5

Mrs. Page. Give your men the charge: we must be
brief.

Mrs. Ford. Marry, as I told you before, John and
Robert, be ready here hard by the brewhouse; and
when I suddenly call you, come forth and without any   10
pause or staggering take this basket on your shoulders.
That done, trudge with it in all haste, and carry it
among the whitsters in Datchet Mead, and there
empty it in the muddy ditch close by the Thames
side.   15

Mrs. Page. You will do it?

Mrs. Ford. I ha' told them over and over; they lack
no direction. Be gone, and come when you are called.

                              [*Exeunt Servants.*]

Mrs. Page. Here comes little Robin.

[*Enter Robin.*]

Mrs. Ford. How now, my eyas-musket! What news   20
with you?

Rob. My master, Sir John, is come in at your back
door, Mistress Ford, and requests your company.

Mrs. Page. You little Jack-a-Lent, have you been
true to us?   25

Rob. Ay, I'll be sworn. My master knows not of
your being here, and hath threatened to put me into

37. **pompion:** pumpkin, also a term for a corpulent person.

38. **turtles from jays:** i.e., devoted wives from wantons.

39. **"Have I caught thee, my heavenly jewel":** a quotation from Sir Philip Sidney's *Astrophel and Stella*.

41. **period:** conclusion; utmost limit.

43. **cog:** deceive; **prate:** utter flattery.

everlasting liberty if I tell you of it; for he swears he'll
turn me away.

Mrs. Page. Thou'rt a good boy: this secrecy of thine   30
shall be a tailor to thee and shall make thee a new
doublet and hose. I'll go hide me.

Mrs. Ford. Do so. Go tell thy master I am alone.
                                        [*Exit Robin.*]
Mistress Page, remember you your cue.

Mrs. Page. I warrant thee. If I do not act it, hiss me.   35
                                        [*Exit.*]
Mrs. Ford. Go to, then: we'll use this unwholesome
humidity, this gross wat'ry pompion; we'll teach him
to know turtles from jays.

[*Enter Falstaff.*]

Fal. "Have I caught thee, my heavenly jewel?"
Why, now let me die, for I have lived long enough.   40
This is the period of my ambition. O this blessed hour!

Mrs. Ford. O sweet Sir John!

Fal. Mistress Ford, I cannot cog, I cannot prate,
Mistress Ford. Now shall I sin in my wish: I would
thy husband were dead. I'll speak it before the best   45
lord: I would make thee my lady.

Mrs. Ford. I your lady, Sir John! Alas, I should be a
pitiful lady!

Fal. Let the court of France show me such another.
I see how thine eye would emulate the diamond.   50

52. **ship tire:** headdress fashioned like a ship; **tire-valiant:** whether this means simply a tire of unusual elegance or refers to one of a particular design is uncertain. The first two quartos read "tire-vellet (velvet)."

52–3. **of Venetian admittance:** fashionable in Venice.

56. **tyrant:** i.e., ranter against tires.

59–60. **if Fortune thy foe were not, Nature thy friend:** i.e., if to her natural advantages of beauty were added the wealth to dress fashionably. "Fortune My Foe" was the name of a popular ballad.

67. **Bucklersbury:** a London street on which were located the shops of grocers and apothecaries.

68. **simple time:** i.e., time when the shops receive supplies of fresh herbs.

73. **Counter:** a London prison; the foul odor emanating from it was notorious.

A fantastic Venetian headdress.
From Cesare Negri, *Nuove inventioni di balli* (1604).

Thou hast the right arched beauty of the brow that
becomes the ship tire, the tire-valiant, or any tire of
Venetian admittance.

Mrs. Ford. A plain kerchief, Sir John: my brows become nothing else, nor that well neither.   55

Fal. Thou art a tyrant to say so: thou wouldst make
an absolute courtier; and the firm fixture of thy foot
would give an excellent motion to thy gait in a semicircled farthingale. I see what thou wert, if Fortune
thy foe were not, Nature thy friend. Come, thou canst   60
not hide it.

Mrs. Ford. Believe me, there's no such thing in me.

Fal. What made me love thee? Let that persuade
thee there's something extraordinary in thee. Come,
I cannot cog and say thou art this and that, like a   65
many of these lisping hawthorn buds that come like
women in men's apparel and smell like Bucklersbury
in simple time. I cannot: but I love thee, none but
thee, and thou deservest it.

Mrs. Ford. Do not betray me, sir. I fear you love   70
Mistress Page.

Fal. Thou mightst as well say I love to walk by the
Counter gate, which is as hateful to me as the reek of
a limekiln.

Mrs. Ford. Well, Heaven knows how I love you;   75
and you shall one day find it.

Fal. Keep in that mind. I'll deserve it.

Mrs. Ford. Nay, I must tell you, so you do; or else I
could not be in that mind.

83. **presently:** at once.
85. **arras:** wall hanging.

A woman in a semicircled farthingale.
From the Trevelyan manuscript commonplace book
(ca. 1608, Folger MS V.b.232).

Rob. [*Within*] Mistress Ford, Mistress Ford! here's   80
Mistress Page at the door, sweating, and blowing, and
looking wildly, and would needs speak with you
presently.

Fal. She shall not see me: I will ensconce me behind the arras.   85

Mrs. Ford. Pray you, do so. She's a very tattling
woman.   [*Falstaff hides himself.*]

[*Enter Mistress Page and Robin.*]

What's the matter? how now!

Mrs. Page. O Mistress Ford, what have you done?
You're shamed, y'are overthrown, y'are undone for-   90
ever!

Mrs. Ford. What's the matter, good Mistress Page?

Mrs. Page. O welladay, Mistress Ford! having an
honest man to your husband, to give him such cause
of suspicion!   95

Mrs. Ford. What cause of suspicion?

Mrs. Page. What cause of suspicion! Out upon you!
How am I mistook in you!

Mrs. Ford. Why, alas, what's the matter?

Mrs. Page. Your husband's coming hither, woman,   100
with all the officers in Windsor, to search for a gentleman that he says is here now in the house, by your
consent, to take an ill advantage of his absence. You
are undone.

110. **clear:** innocent.
111. **friend:** lover; **amazed:** paralyzed.
113. **good life:** respectability.
125. **whiting:** bleaching.

Mrs. Ford. 'Tis not so, I hope.   105

Mrs. Page. Pray Heaven it be not so, that you have
such a man here! But 'tis most certain your husband's
coming, with half Windsor at his heels, to search for
such a one. I come before to tell you. If you know
yourself clear, why, I am glad of it; but if you have   110
a friend here, convey, convey him out. Be not amazed;
call all your senses to you; defend your reputation, or
bid farewell to your good life forever.

Mrs. Ford. What shall I do? There is a gentleman
my dear friend; and I fear not mine own shame so   115
much as his peril. I had rather than a thousand pound
he were out of the house.

Mrs. Page. For shame! Never stand "you had
rather" and "you had rather." Your husband's here at
hand; bethink you of some conveyance. In the house   120
you cannot hide him. O, how have you deceived me!
Look, here is a basket: if he be of any reasonable
stature, he may creep in here; and throw foul linen
upon him, as if it were going to bucking: or—it is
whiting time—send him by your two men to Datchet   125
Mead.

Mrs. Ford. He's too big to go in there. What shall
I do?

Fal. [*Coming forward*] Let me see't, let me see't,
O, let me see't! I'll in, I'll in! Follow your friend's   130
counsel. I'll in!

Mrs. Page. What, Sir John Falstaff! Are these your
letters, knight?

140. **cowlstaff:** pole on which to sling the basket so that two could carry it; **drumble:** loiter; dawdle.

147. **what have you to do:** what business is it of yours.

149–50. **wash myself of the buck:** i.e., rid himself of the fear of being a cuckold.

151. **buck, and of the season;** the buck is Falstaff; **the season** is rutting time.

Fal. I love thee. Help me away. Let me creep in
here. I'll never—   135
[*Gets into the basket; they cover him with foul linen.*]

Mrs. Page. Help to cover your master, boy. Call
your men, Mistress Ford. You dissembling knight!

Mrs. Ford. What, John! Robert! John! [*Exit Robin.*]

[*Enter Servants.*]

Go take up these clothes here quickly. Where's the
cowlstaff? Look how you drumble! Carry them to the   140
laundress in Datchet Mead. Quickly, come!

[*Enter Ford, Page, Caius, and Sir Hugh Evans.*]

Ford. Pray you, come near. If I suspect without
cause, why then make sport at me; then let me be
your jest: I deserve it. How now! Whither bear you
this?   145

Ser. To the laundress, forsooth.

Mrs. Ford. Why, what have you to do whither they
bear it? You were best meddle with buck washing.

Ford. Buck! I would I could wash myself of the
buck! Buck, buck, buck! Ay, buck; I warrant you,   150
buck, and of the season too, it shall appear. [*Exeunt
Servants with the basket.*] Gentlemen, I have dreamed
tonight: I'll tell you my dream. Here, here, here be
my keys: ascend my chambers; search, seek, find out.

179. **gross:** obvious.

62

I'll warrant we'll unkennel the fox. Let me stop this 155
way first. [*Locking the door.*] So, now uncape.

Page. Good Master Ford, be contented: you wrong
yourself too much.

Ford. True, Master Page. Up, gentlemen: you shall
see sport anon. Follow me, gentlemen.   [*Exit.*] 160

Evans. This is fery fantastical humors and jealousies.

Caius. By gar, 'tis no the fashion of France. It is not
jealous in France.

Page. Nay, follow him, gentlemen. See the issue of 165
his search.   [*Exeunt Page, Caius, and Evans.*]

Mrs. Page. Is there not a double excellency in this?

Mrs. Ford. I know not which pleases me better, that
my husband is deceived, or Sir John.

Mrs. Page. What a taking was he in when your hus- 170
band asked who was in the basket!

Mrs. Ford. I am half afraid he will have need of
washing, so throwing him into the water will do him
a benefit.

Mrs. Page. Hang him, dishonest rascal! I would all 175
of the same strain were in the same distress.

Mrs. Ford. I think my husband hath some special
suspicion of Falstaff's being here, for I never saw him
so gross in his jealousy till now.

Mrs. Page. I will lay a plot to try that; and we will 180
yet have more tricks with Falstaff. His dissolute dis-
ease will scarce obey this medicine.

183. **carrion:** disreputable woman.
190. **compass:** achieve.
197. **do yourself . . . wrong:** disgrace yourself.
201. **presses:** cupboards.
206. **your distemper in this kind:** this ailment
that so afflicts you.
208. **fault:** misfortune.

Mrs. Ford. Shall we send that foolish carrion, Mistress Quickly, to him, and excuse his throwing into the water, and give him another hope, to betray him 185 to another punishment?

Mrs. Page. We will do it. Let him be sent for to-morrow, eight o'clock, to have amends.

[*Enter Ford, Page, Caius, and Sir Hugh Evans.*]

Ford. I cannot find him; maybe the knave bragged of that he could not compass. 190

Mrs. Page. [*Aside to Mrs. Ford*] Heard you that?

Mrs. Ford. You use me well, Master Ford, do you?

Ford. Ay, I do so.

Mrs. Ford. Heaven make you better than your thoughts! 195

Ford. Amen!

Mrs. Page. You do yourself mighty wrong, Master Ford.

Ford. Ay, ay. I must bear it.

Evans. If there be anybody in the house, and in the 200 chambers, and in the coffers, and in the presses, Heaven forgive my sins at the Day of Judgment!

Caius. Be-gar, nor I too. There is nobodies.

Page. Fie, fie, Master Ford! are you not ashamed? What spirit, what devil suggests this imagination? I 205 would not ha' your distemper in this kind for the wealth of Windsor Castle.

Ford. 'Tis my fault, Master Page: I suffer for it.

221. for the bush: i.e., suitable for hunting small birds among bushes.

Hawking.
From Erasmo di Valvasone, *La caccia* (ca. 1602).

Evans. You suffer for a pad conscience. Your wife is as honest a omans as I will desires among five thou- 210 sand, and five hundred too.

Caius. By gar, I see 'tis an honest woman.

Ford. Well, I promised you a dinner. Come, come, walk in the park. I pray you, pardon me: I will here- after make known to you why I have done this. 215 Come, wife; come, Mistress Page. I pray you, pardon me; pray heartily pardon me.

Page. Let's go in, gentlemen, but, trust me, we'll mock him. I do invite you tomorrow morning to my house to breakfast. After, we'll a-birding together. I 220 have a fine hawk for the bush. Shall it be so?

Ford. Anything.

Evans. If there is one, I shall make two in the company.

Caius. If there be one or two, I shall make-a the 225 turd.

Ford. Pray you, go, Master Page.

Evans. I pray you now, remembrance tomorrow on the lousy knave, mine host.

Caius. Dat is good; by gar, with all my heart!   230

Evans. A lousy knave, to have his gibes and his mockeries.

                                              Exeunt.

III.iv. Fenton expresses to Anne Page his despair of gaining her father's favor, and Anne counsels him not to give up the attempt. Quickly and Shallow escort Slender to court Anne, but he reveals himself an unenthusiastic suitor. Page and Mrs. Page enter and Page orders Fenton to depart and pay no more visits to his daughter. Fenton tries to win Mrs. Page's support; although she favors Dr. Caius, she pretends to be impartial and agreeable to accepting the man most pleasing to Anne.

░░░░░░░░░░░░░░░░░░░░░░░░░

6. **my state being galled:** my estate being damaged.

8. **bars:** objections.

17. **stamps in gold:** gold coins.

Scene IV. [A room in Page's house.]

Enter Fenton and Anne Page.

Fen. I see I cannot get thy father's love;
Therefore no more turn me to him, sweet Nan.
 Anne. Alas, how then?
 Fen.   Why, thou must be thyself.
He doth object I am too great of birth;   5
And that, my state being galled with my expense,
I seek to heal it only by his wealth.
Besides these, other bars he lays before me,
My riots past, my wild societies;
And tells me 'tis a thing impossible   10
I should love thee but as a property.
 Anne. Maybe he tells you true.
 Fen. No, Heaven so speed me in my time to come!
Albeit I will confess thy father's wealth
Was the first motive that I wooed thee, Anne.   15
Yet, wooing thee, I found thee of more value
Than stamps in gold or sums in sealed bags;
And 'tis the very riches of thyself
That now I aim at.
 Anne.   Gentle Master Fenton,   20
Yet seek my father's love; still seek it, sir:

26. **a shaft or a bolt on't:** a sharp or blunt missile of it; that is, he'll try, although he may not succeed; **'Slid:** God's eyelid.

39–40. **thou hadst a father:** i.e., act like a man.

If opportunity and humblest suit
Cannot attain it, why, then—hark you hither!

　　　　　　　　　　[They converse apart.]

　[Enter Shallow, Slender, and Mistress Quickly.]

　Shal. Break their talk, Mistress Quickly: my kins-
man shall speak for himself.　　　　　　　　　　25

　Slen. I'll make a shaft or a bolt on't. 'Slid, 'tis but
venturing.

　Shal. Be not dismayed.

　Slen. No, she shall not dismay me: I care not for
that, but that I am afeard.　　　　　　　　　　30

　Quick. Hark ye, Master Slender would speak a
word with you.

　Anne. I come to him. *[Aside]* This is my father's
　　choice.

O, what a world of vile, ill-favored faults　　　35
Looks handsome in three hundred pounds a year!

　Quick. And how does good Master Fenton? Pray
you, a word with you.

　Shal. She's coming: to her, coz. O boy, thou hadst a
father!　　　　　　　　　　40

　Slen. I had a father, Mistress Anne. My uncle can
tell you good jests of him. Pray you, uncle, tell Mistress Anne the jest, how my father stole two geese out
of a pen, good uncle.

　Shal. Mistress Anne, my cousin loves you.　　　45

49. **cut and longtail:** curtailed and long-tailed dogs. The expression is common.

52. **jointure:** marriage settlement.

60. **Od's heartlings:** God's little heart.

67-8. **happy man be his dole:** proverbial, "may the winner be a happy man."

Slen. Ay, that I do, as well as I love any woman in
Gloucestershire.

Shal. He will maintain you like a gentlewoman.

Slen. Ay, that I will, come cut and longtail, under
the degree of a squire.   50

Shal. He will make you a hundred and fifty pounds
jointure.

Anne. Good Master Shallow, let him woo for himself.

Shal. Marry, I thank you for it. I thank you for that   55
good comfort. She calls you, coz. I'll leave you.

Anne. Now, Master Slender.

Slen. Now, good Mistress Anne.

Anne. What is your will?

Slen. My will! Od's heartlings, that's a pretty jest   60
indeed! I ne'er made my will yet, I thank Heaven: I
am not such a sickly creature, I give Heaven praise.

Anne. I mean, Master Slender, what would you
with me?

Slen. Truly, for mine own part, I would little or   65
nothing with you. Your father and my uncle hath
made motions. If it be my luck, so; if not, happy man
be his dole! They can tell you how things go better
than I can. You may ask your father: here he comes.

[*Enter Page and Mistress Page.*]

Page. Now, Master Slender. Love him, daughter   70
Anne.

84. **for that:** because.

87. **Perforce:** whether I wish to or not.

88. **advance the colors:** raise the flag (a battle signal).

94. **quick:** alive.

Why, how now! What does Master Fenton here?
You wrong me, sir, thus still to haunt my house.
I told you, sir, my daughter is disposed of.

    Fen. Nay, Master Page, be not impatient.   75

    Mrs. Page. Good Master Fenton, come not to my
      child.

    Page. She is no match for you.

    Fen. Sir, will you hear me?

    Page.   No, good Master Fenton. 80
Come, Master Shallow; come, son Slender, in.
Knowing my mind, you wrong me, Master Fenton.

         [*Exeunt Page, Shallow, and Slender.*]

    Quick. Speak to Mistress Page.

    Fen. Good Mistress Page, for that I love your
      daughter   85
In such a righteous fashion as I do,
Perforce, against all checks, rebukes and manners,
I must advance the colors of my love,
And not retire. Let me have your good will.

    Anne. Good mother, do not marry me to yond fool. 90

    Mrs. Page. I mean it not: I seek you a better hus-
band.

    Quick. That's my master, Master Doctor.

    Anne. Alas, I had rather be set quick i' the earth,
And bowled to death with turnips!   95

    Mrs. Page. Come, trouble not yourself. Good Mas-
      ter Fenton,
I will not be your friend nor enemy.

107. **once:** at some time.
116. **speciously:** especially; **of:** i.e., go on.

My daughter will I question how she loves you,
And as I find her, so am I affected.   100
Till then farewell, sir: she must needs go in.
Her father will be angry.

    Fen. Farewell, gentle mistress: farewell, Nan.

                [Exeunt Mrs. Page and Anne.]

    Quick. This is my doing now. "Nay," said I, "will
you cast away your child on a fool, and a physician? 105
Look on Master Fenton." This is my doing.

    Fen. I thank thee; and I pray thee, once tonight
Give my sweet Nan this ring. There's for thy pains.

    Quick. Now Heaven send thee good fortune!

                    [Exit Fenton.]

A kind heart he hath: a woman would run through 110
fire and water for such a kind heart. But yet I would
my master had Mistress Anne; or I would Master
Slender had her; or, in sooth, I would Master Fenton
had her. I will do what I can for them all three; for so
I have promised, and I'll be as good as my word; but 115
speciously for Master Fenton. Well, I must of another
errand to Sir John Falstaff from my two mistresses.
What a beast am I to slack it!

                            Exit.

III.v. Falstaff indignantly relates his humiliation at being dumped into the Thames from the clothes basket. But when Quickly brings another invitation from Mrs. Ford, he agrees to visit her again while her husband is birding. Ford himself, in the character of Brook, comes to learn of Falstaff's luck with Mrs. Ford, and Falstaff reports the new assignation, revealing at the same time how he was thwarted at his last meeting. Ford is certain that this time he will catch Falstaff with his wife.

‖‖‖‖‖‖‖‖‖‖‖‖‖‖‖‖‖‖‖‖‖‖‖‖‖‖

3. **toast:** piece of toasted bread as a sop.

9. **slighted:** threw contemptuously; **remorse:** pity; compassion.

18. **mummy:** dead flesh.

Scene V. [A room in the Garter Inn.]

Enter Falstaff and Bardolph.

Fal. Bardolph, I say—
Bar. Here, sir.
Fal. Go fetch me a quart of sack; put a toast in't.
[*Exit Bardolph.*] Have I lived to be carried in a basket, like a barrow of butcher's offal, and to be thrown   5
in the Thames? Well, if I be served such another trick,
I'll have my brains ta'en out and buttered, and give
them to a dog for a New Year's gift. The rogues
slighted me into the river with as little remorse as
they would have drowned a blind bitch's puppies, fif-   10
teen i' the litter; and you may know by my size that
I have a kind of alacrity in sinking. If the bottom
were as deep as hell, I should down. I had been
drowned but that the shore was shelvy and shallow
—a death that I abhor, for the water swells a man,   15
and what a thing should I have been when I had
been swelled! I should have been a mountain of
mummy.

[*Enter Bardolph with sack.*]

Bar. Here's Mistress Quickly, sir, to speak with
you.   20
Fal. Come, let me pour in some sack to the Thames
water; for my belly's as cold as if I had swallowed

23. **reins:** kidneys.
25. **cry you mercy:** beg your pardon.
30. **Simple of itself:** undiluted.
38. **erection:** mistake for "direction."
42. **yearn:** grieve.
44. **between eight and nine:** the time references seem to be confused, unless Falstaff is conceived as having been out all night.

snowballs for pills to cool the reins. Call her in.

Bar. Come in, woman!

[Enter Mistress Quickly.]

Quick. By your leave. I cry you mercy. Give your   25
Worship good morrow.

Fal. Take away these chalices. Go brew me a pottle
of sack finely.

Bar. With eggs, sir?

Fal. Simple of itself. I'll no pullet sperm in my brew-   30
age. *[Exit Bardolph.]* How now!

Quick. Marry, sir, I come to your Worship from
Mistress Ford.

Fal. Mistress Ford! I have had ford enough. I was
thrown into the ford. I have my belly full of ford.   35

Quick. Alas the day! Good heart, that was not her
fault. She does so take on with her men: they mistook
their erection.

Fal. So did I mine, to build upon a foolish woman's
promise.   40

Quick. Well, she laments, sir, for it, that it would
yearn your heart to see it. Her husband goes this
morning a-birding. She desires you once more to
come to her between eight and nine. I must carry her
word quickly. She'll make you amends, I warrant you.   45

Fal. Well, I will visit her: tell her so. And bid her
think what a man is: let her consider his frailty and
then judge of my merit.

Quick. I will tell her.

52. **miss:** fail.

67. **peaking:** prying; **cornuto:** Italian for "cuckold."

69–70. **encounter:** amorous meeting.

Fal. Do so. Between nine and ten, sayst thou?   50
Quick. Eight and nine, sir.
Fal. Well, be gone. I will not miss her.
Quick. Peace be with you, sir.   [*Exit.*]
Fal. I marvel I hear not of Master Brook. He sent
me word to stay within. I like his money well. O, here   55
he comes.

[*Enter Ford.*]

Ford. Bless you, sir!
Fal. Now, Master Brook, you come to know what
hath passed between me and Ford's wife?
Ford. That, indeed, Sir John, is my business.   60
Fal. Master Brook, I will not lie to you: I was at her
house the hour she appointed me.
Ford. And sped you, sir?
Fal. Very ill-favoredly, Master Brook.
Ford. How so, sir? Did she change her determina-   65
tion?
Fal. No, Master Brook, but the peaking cornuto
her husband, Master Brook, dwelling in a continual
'larum of jealousy, comes me in the instant of our encounter, after we had embraced, kissed, protested,   70
and, as it were, spoke the prologue of our comedy;
and at his heels a rabble of his companions, thither
provoked and instigated by his distemper, and, forsooth, to search his house for his wife's love.
Ford. What, while you were there?   75
Fal. While I was there.

86. **smocks:** ladies' shifts.

93. **knaves . . . hinds:** menials.

104. **bellwether:** castrated male leader of a flock of sheep; **compassed:** surrounded.

Ford. And did he search for you and could not find
you?

Fal. You shall hear. As good luck would have it,
comes in one Mistress Page; gives intelligence of   80
Ford's approach; and, in her invention and Ford's
wife's distraction, they conveyed me into a buck basket.

Ford. A buck basket!

Fal. Yes, a buck basket!—rammed me in with foul   85
shirts and smocks, socks, foul stockings, greasy nap-
kins; that, Master Brook, there was the rankest com-
pound of villainous smell that ever offended nostril.

Ford. And how long lay you there?

Fal. Nay, you shall hear, Master Brook, what I   90
have suffered to bring this woman to evil for your
good. Being thus crammed in the basket, a couple of
Ford's knaves, his hinds, were called forth by their
mistress to carry me in the name of foul clothes to
Datchet Lane. They took me on their shoulders; met   95
the jealous knave their master in the door, who asked
them once or twice what they had in their basket. I
quaked for fear lest the lunatic knave would have
searched it; but fate, ordaining he should be a cuckold, held his hand. Well, on went he for a search, and   100
away went I for foul clothes. But mark the sequel,
Master Brook. I suffered the pangs of three several
deaths: first, an intolerable fright, to be detected with
a jealous, rotten bellwether; next, to be compassed,
like a good bilbo, in the circumference of a peck, hilt   105
to point, heel to head; and then, to be stopped in, like

107. **fretted:** chafed.
108–109. **kidney:** constitution.
111. **in the height of:** on top of.
117. **In good sadness:** most sincerely.
123. **embassy:** message.
126. **address me to:** prepare myself for.

a strong distillation, with stinking clothes that fretted
in their own grease. Think of that, a man of my kidney—think of that—that am as subject to heat as butter; a man of continual dissolution and thaw. It was a   110
miracle to 'scape suffocation. And in the height of this
bath, when I was more than half stewed in grease,
like a Dutch dish, to be thrown into the Thames and
cooled, glowing hot, in that surge, like a horseshoe!
Think of that—hissing hot!—think of that, Master   115
Brook!

Ford. In good sadness, sir, I am sorry that for my
sake you have suffered all this. My suit, then, is des-
perate? You'll undertake her no more?

Fal. Master Brook, I will be thrown into Etna, as I   120
have been into Thames, ere I will leave her thus. Her
husband is this morning gone a-birding. I have received from her another embassy of meeting: 'twixt
eight and nine is the hour, Master Brook.

Ford. 'Tis past eight already, sir.   125

Fal. Is it? I will then address me to my appointment. Come to me at your convenient leisure and you
shall know how I speed; and the conclusion shall be
crowned with your enjoying her. Adieu. You shall
have her, Master Brook. Master Brook, you shall   130
cuckold Ford.   [*Exit.*]

Ford. Hum! ha! Is this a vision? Is this a dream?
Do I sleep? Master Ford, awake! Awake, Master
Ford! There's a hole made in your best coat, Master
Ford. This 'tis to be married! This 'tis to have linen   135
and buck baskets! Well, I will proclaim myself what

I am. I will now take the lecher. He is at my house:
he cannot scape me; 'tis impossible he should. He
cannot creep into a halfpenny purse nor into a pep-
per box; but, lest the devil that guides him should   140
aid him, I will search impossible places. Though what
I am I cannot avoid, yet to be what I would not shall
not make me tame. If I have horns to make one mad,
let the proverb go with me: I'll be horn-mad.

                                             Exit.

THE
MERRY WIVES
OF
WINDSOR

ACT IV

IV.i. Quickly informs Mrs. Page of Falstaff's tryst with Mrs. Ford and urges her to join her confederate. Before they set out Mrs. Page has Sir Hugh test her son's knowledge of Latin.

⁓⁓⁓⁓⁓⁓⁓⁓⁓⁓⁓⁓⁓⁓⁓⁓⁓⁓⁓⁓⁓⁓⁓⁓⁓⁓⁓⁓

4. **courageous:** outrageous.
16. **accidence:** Latin grammar.

ACT IV

Scene I. [A Windsor street.]

Enter Mistress Page, Quickly, and William.

Mrs. Page. Is he at Master Ford's already, thinkst thou?

Quick. Sure he is by this, or will be presently; but, truly, he is very courageous mad about his throwing into the water. Mistress Ford desires you to come sud- 5 denly.

Mrs. Page. I'll be with her by and by. I'll but bring my young man here to school. Look where his master comes. 'Tis a playing day, I see.

[*Enter Sir Hugh Evans.*]

How now, Sir Hugh! no school today? 10

Evans. No. Master Slender is let the boys leave to play.

Quick. Blessing of his heart!

Mrs. Page. Sir Hugh, my husband says my son prof- its nothing in the world at his book. I pray you, ask 15 him some questions in his accidence.

24. **Od's nouns:** corruption of "God's wounds."
28. **Polecats:** slang for "harlots."

Evans. Come hither, William. Hold up your head; come.

Mrs. Page. Come on, sirrah. Hold up your head: answer your master, be not afraid.   20

Evans. William, how many numbers is in nouns?

Will. Two.

Quick. Truly, I thought there had been one number more, because they say, "Od's nouns."

Evans. Peace your tattlings! What is "fair," Wil- 25
liam?

Will. Pulcher.

Quick. Polecats! There are fairer things than polecats, sure.

Evans. You are a very simplicity oman: I pray you, 30
peace. What is *lapis,* William?

Will. A stone.

Evans. And what is a stone, William?

Will. A pebble.

Evans. No, it is *lapis:* I pray you, remember in your 35
prain.

Will. Lapis.

Evans. That is a good William. What is he, William, that does lend articles?

Will. Articles are borrowed of the pronoun, and be 40
thus declined, *singulariter, nominativo, hic, haec, hoc.*

Evans. Nominativo, *hig, hag, hog;* pray you, mark:
genitivo, hujus. Well, what is your accusative case?

Will. Accusativo, *hinc.*

Evans. I pray you, have your remembrance, child: 45
accusativo, hung, hang, hog.

51. **caret:** omitted.
75. **preeches:** breeched; i.e., whipped.

Quick. Hang-hog is Latin for bacon, I warrant you.

Evans. Leave your prabbles, oman. What is the focative case, William?

Will. O, *vocativo*, O.   50

Evans. Remember, William: focative is *caret*.

Quick. And that's a good root.

Evans. Oman, forbear.

Mrs. Page. Peace!

Evans. What is your genitive case plural, William?   55

Will. Genitive case?

Evans. Ay.

Will. Genitive: *horum, harum, horum.*

Quick. Vengeance of Jinny's case! Fie on her! Never name her, child, if she be a whore.   60

Evans. For shame, oman.

Quick. You do ill to teach the child such words. He teaches him to hick and to hack, which they'll do fast enough of themselves, and to call *horum*. Fie upon you!   65

Evans. Oman, art thou lunatics? Hast thou no understandings for thy cases and the numbers of the genders? Thou art as foolish Christian creatures as I would desires.

Mrs. Page. [*To Quickly*] Prithee, hold thy peace.   70

Evans. Show me now, William, some declensions of your pronouns.

Will. Forsooth, I have forgot.

Evans. It is *qui, quae, quod*: if you forget your *quis*, your *quaes*, and your *quods*, you must be preeches.   75
Go your ways, and play: go!

79. **sprag:** sprack; sprightly.

━━━━━━━━━━━━━━━━━━━━━━━

IV.ii. In accordance with their plan, Mrs. Page interrupts Falstaff and Mrs. Ford to report that Ford, in a jealous rage, is returning to surprise her. The clothes basket will not do for a second escape, so they dress Falstaff as an old woman of unsavory reputation. The basket, this time full of nothing but clothes, attracts Ford's attention and gains the women time to dress Falstaff. Frustrated at not finding his quarry, Ford vents his anger on the supposed old woman and beats her out of the house. Mrs. Ford and Mrs. Page feel that Falstaff should have learned his lesson by this time, and they resolve to tell their husbands the whole story and let them decide whether they should torment the fat knight any further.

━━━━━━━━━━━━━━━━━━━━━━━

2. **sufferance:** suffering; **obsequious:** devoted.
4-5. **accouterment, complement, and ceremony:** i.e., courteous formalities that attend love.
8. **gossip:** a term for a confidential friend.

Mrs. Page. He is a better scholar than I thought he was.

Evans. He is a good sprag memory. Farewell, Mistress Page.   80

Mrs. Page. Adieu, good Sir Hugh. [*Exit Sir Hugh.*] Get you home, boy. Come, we stay too long.

Exeunt.

Scene II. [A room in Ford's house.]

Enter Falstaff and Mistress Ford.

Fal. Mistress Ford, your sorrow hath eaten up my sufferance. I see you are obsequious in your love, and I profess requital to a hair's breadth, not only, Mistress Ford, in the simple office of love, but in all the accouterment, complement, and ceremony of it. But   5 are you sure of your husband now?

Mrs. Ford. He's a-birding, sweet Sir John.

Mrs. Page. [*Within*] What, ho, gossip Ford! What, ho!

Mrs. Ford. Step into the chamber, Sir John.   10
[*Exit Falstaff.*]

[*Enter Mistress Page.*]

Mrs. Page. How now, sweetheart! who's at home besides yourself?

Mrs. Ford. Why, none but mine own people.

23. complexion: disposition.

Mrs. Page. Indeed!

Mrs. Ford. No, certainly. [*Aside to her*] Speak   15
louder.

Mrs. Page. Truly, I am so glad you have nobody
here.

Mrs. Ford. Why?

Mrs. Page. Why, woman, your husband is in his   20
old lines again. He so takes on yonder with my husband, so rails against all married mankind, so curses
all Eve's daughters, of what complexion soever, and
so buffets himself on the forehead, crying, "Peer out,
peer out!" that any madness I ever yet beheld seemed   25
but tameness, civility, and patience to this his distemper he is in now. I am glad the fat knight is not
here.

Mrs. Ford. Why, does he talk of him?

Mrs. Page. Of none but him, and swears he was   30
carried out, the last time he searched for him, in a
basket; protests to my husband he is now here; and
hath drawn him and the rest of their company from
their sport, to make another experiment of his suspicion. But I am glad the knight is not here. Now he   35
shall see his own foolery.

Mrs. Ford. How near is he, Mistress Page?

Mrs. Page. Hard by, at street end. He will be here
anon.

Mrs. Ford. I am undone! The knight is here.   40

Mrs. Page. Why, then, you are utterly shamed, and
he's but a dead man. What a woman are you! Away
with him, away with him! Better shame than murder.

58. **abstract:** i.e., list (for inventory purposes).

67. **muffler:** cloth worn over the mouth, also known as a "chinclout."

70. **mischief:** injury.

A Country Woman

A countrywoman with a muffler over her mouth.
From John Speed, *Theatrum imperii Magnae Britanniae* (1616).

Mrs. Ford. Which way should he go? How should
I bestow him? Shall I put him into the basket again?   45

[*Enter Falstaff.*]

Fal. No, I'll come no more i' the basket. May I not
go out ere he come?

Mrs. Page. Alas, three of Master Ford's brothers
watch the door with pistols, that none shall issue out:
otherwise you might slip away ere he came. But what   50
make you here?

Fal. What shall I do? I'll creep up into the chimney.

Mrs. Ford. There they always use to discharge their
birding pieces. Creep into the kiln hole.

Fal. Where is it?   55

Mrs. Ford. He will seek there, on my word. Neither
press, coffer, chest, trunk, well, vault, but he hath an
abstract for the remembrance of such places and goes
to them by his note. There is no hiding you in the
house.   60

Fal. I'll go out, then.

Mrs. Page. If you go out in your own semblance,
you die, Sir John—unless you go out disguised.

Mrs. Ford. How might we disguise him?

Mrs. Page. Alas the day, I know not! There is no   65
woman's gown big enough for him: otherwise he
might put on a hat, a muffler, and a kerchief, and so
escape.

Fal. Good hearts, devise something. Any extremity
rather than a mischief.   70

74. **thrummed hat:** a hat made of "thrums," short ends or tufts of wool.

77. **look:** seek.

79. **straight:** immediately.

87. **in good sadness:** truly.

Mrs. Ford. My maid's aunt, the fat woman of Brainford, has a gown above.

Mrs. Page. On my word, it will serve him: she's as
big as he is. And there's her thrummed hat, and her
muffler too. Run up, Sir John.   75

Mrs. Ford. Go, go, sweet Sir John. Mistress Page
and I will look some linen for your head.

Mrs. Page. Quick, quick! We'll come dress you
straight. Put on the gown the while.   [*Exit Falstaff.*]

Mrs. Ford. I would my husband would meet him in   80
this shape. He cannot abide the old woman of Brainford: he swears she's a witch, forbade her my house,
and hath threatened to beat her.

Mrs. Page. Heaven guide him to thy husband's
cudgel, and the Devil guide his cudgel afterwards!   85

Mrs. Ford. But is my husband coming?

Mrs. Page. Ay, in good sadness, is he, and talks of
the basket too, howsoever he hath had intelligence.

Mrs. Ford. We'll try that: for I'll appoint my men to
carry the basket again, to meet him at the door with   90
it, as they did last time.

Mrs. Page. Nay, but he'll be here presently. Let's go
dress him like the witch of Brainford.

Mrs. Ford. I'll first direct my men what they shall
do with the basket. Go up. I'll bring linen for him   95
straight.   [*Exit.*]

Mrs. Page. Hang him, dishonest varlet! We cannot
misuse him enough.
We'll leave a proof, by that which we will do,
Wives may be merry and yet honest too.   100

102. **Still swine eats all the draff:** an old proverb warning against trusting those who seem quiet and well behaved.

110. **unfool me:** help me lose the appellation "fool."

112. **ging:** gang.

113. **pack:** group of conspirators.

113–14. **Now shall the Devil be shamed:** i.e., by revelation of the truth, referring to the proverb "Tell truth and shame the Devil."

117. **passes:** surpasses; exceeds everything.

We do not act that often jest and laugh;
'Tis old, but true: Still swine eats all the draff. [*Exit.*]

[*Enter Mistress Ford with two Servants.*]

Mrs. Ford. Go, sirs, take the basket again on your
shoulders. Your master is hard at door. If he bid you
set it down, obey him. Quickly, dispatch!   [*Exit.*] 105
    1. Ser. Come, come, take it up.
    2. Ser. Pray Heaven it be not full of knight again.
    1. Ser. I hope not: I had as lief bear so much lead.

[*Enter Ford, Page, Shallow, Caius, and
Sir Hugh Evans.*]

Ford. Ay, but if it prove true, Master Page, have
you any way then to unfool me again? Set down the 110
basket, villain! Somebody call my wife. Youth in a
basket! O you panderly rascals! There's a knot, a ging,
a pack, a conspiracy against me. Now shall the Devil
be shamed. What, wife, I say! Come, come forth!
Behold what honest clothes you send forth to bleach- 115
ing!
    Page. Why, this passes, Master Ford! You are not
to go loose any longer: you must be pinioned.
    Evans. Why, this is lunatics! This is mad as a mad
dog!   120
    Shal. Indeed, Master Ford, this is not well, indeed.
    Ford. So say I too, sir.

142. **jealousy:** suspicion.
147. **fidelity:** faith.
148. **wrongs:** disgraces.

[*Enter Mistress Ford.*]

Come hither, Mistress Ford! Mistress Ford, the
honest woman, the modest wife, the virtuous creature,
that hath the jealous fool to her husband! I suspect   125
without cause, mistress, do I?

Mrs. Ford. Heaven be my witness you do, if you
suspect me in any dishonesty.

Ford. Well said, brazen-face! Hold it out. Come
forth, sirrah!   [*Pulling clothes out of the basket.*]   130

Page. This passes!

Mrs. Ford. Are you not ashamed? Let the clothes
alone.

Ford. I shall find you anon.

Evans. 'Tis unreasonable! Will you take up your   135
wife's clothes? Come away.

Ford. Empty the basket, I say!

Mrs. Ford. Why, man, why?

Ford. Master Page, as I am a man, there was one
conveyed out of my house yesterday in this basket.   140
Why may not he be there again? In my house I am
sure he is. My intelligence is true; my jealousy is
reasonable. Pluck me out all the linen.

Mrs. Ford. If you find a man there, he shall die a
flea's death.   145

Page. Here's no man.

Shal. By my fidelity, this is not well, Master Ford:
this wrongs you.

Evans. Master Ford, you must pray, and not follow

154. **show no color:** offer no excuse.

157. **leman:** lover.

164. **quean:** disreputable woman; **cozening:** cheating.

165. **of:** on.

169. **the figure:** astronomical signs; **daub'ry:** hocus-pocus.

the imaginations of your own heart. This is jealousies.   150

Ford. Well, he's not here I seek for.

Page. No, nor nowhere else but in your brain.

Ford. Help to search my house this one time. If I
find not what I seek, show no color for my extremity:
let me forever be your table sport. Let them say of me,   155
"As jealous as Ford, that searched a hollow walnut for
his wife's leman." Satisfy me once more. Once more
search with me.

Mrs. Ford. What, ho, Mistress Page! Come you and
the old woman down: my husband will come into   160
the chamber.

Ford. Old woman! What old woman's that?

Mrs. Ford. Why, it is my maid's aunt of Brainford.

Ford. A witch, a quean, an old cozening quean!
Have I not forbid her my house? She comes of   165
errands, does she? We are simple men: we do not
know what's brought to pass under the profession of
fortunetelling. She works by charms, by spells, by
the figure, and such daub'ry as this is, beyond our
element: we know nothing. Come down, you witch,   170
you hag, you! Come down, I say!

Mrs. Ford. Nay, good, sweet husband! Good gentlemen, let him not strike the old woman.

[*Enter Falstaff in woman's clothes, and
Mistress Page.*]

Mrs. Page. Come, Mother Prat, come, give me your
hand.   175

176. **prat her:** beat her on the bottom.

178. **ronyon:** literally, a scabby person; slattern.

185. **peard:** a beard on a woman was considered evidence that she was a witch.

188–89. **If I cry out thus upon no trail, never trust me when I open again:** a metaphor from hunting with hounds.

201. **in fee simple:** a law term signifying unconditional ownership.

Ford. I'll prat her. [*Beating him*] Out of my door,
you witch, you rag, you baggage, you polecat, you
ronyon! Out, out! I'll conjure you, I'll fortunetell you.
[*Exit Falstaff.*]

Mrs. Page. Are you not ashamed? I think you have
killed the poor woman.   180

Mrs. Ford. Nay, he will do it. 'Tis a goodly credit
for you.

Ford. Hang her, witch!

Evans. By yea and no, I think the oman is a witch
indeed: I like not when a oman has a great peard. I 185
spy a great peard under her muffler.

Ford. Will you follow, gentlemen? I beseech you,
follow. See but the issue of my jealousy. If I cry out
thus upon no trail, never trust me when I open again.

Page. Let's obey his humor a little further. Come, 190
gentlemen.

[*Exeunt Ford, Page, Shallow, Caius, and Evans.*]

Mrs. Page. Trust me, he beat him most pitifully.

Mrs. Ford. Nay, by the mass, that he did not: he
beat him most unpitifully methought.

Mrs. Page. I'll have the cudgel hallowed and hung 195
o'er the altar. It hath done meritorious service.

Mrs. Ford. What think you? May we, with the warrant of womanhood and the witness of a good conscience, pursue him with any further revenge?

Mrs. Page. The spirit of wantonness is, sure, scared 200
out of him. If the Devil have him not in fee simple,

202. **fine and recovery:** a method for the conveyance of property.

202–3. **in the way of waste:** as though they were common land, subject to exploitation by anyone.

207. **figures:** suspicious imaginings.

210. **ministers:** agents.

212. **period:** conclusion.

214–15. **to the forge with it . . . I would not have things cool:** Mrs. Page remembers the proverbial warning to strike while the iron is hot.

▬▬▬▬▬▬▬▬▬▬▬▬▬▬▬▬▬▬▬

IV.iii. Bardolph reports to the host that the party of a German duke seeks horses, and the host promises that they shall pay well for them.

▬▬▬▬▬▬▬▬▬▬▬▬▬

2. **The Duke:** Count Mömpelgart, later Duke of Württemberg, visited England in 1592. His pompous arrogance made him unpopular. For several years afterward he eagerly sought to be made a Knight of the Garter, an honor which was at last accorded him in 1597.

with fine and recovery, he will never, I think, in the
way of waste, attempt us again.

Mrs. Ford. Shall we tell our husbands how we
have served him?   205

Mrs. Page. Yes, by all means, if it be but to scrape
the figures out of your husband's brains. If they can
find in their hearts the poor, unvirtuous, fat knight
shall be any further afflicted, we two will still be the
ministers.   210

Mrs. Ford. I'll warrant they'll have him publicly
shamed: and methinks there would be no period to
the jest, should he not be publicly shamed.

Mrs. Page. Come, to the forge with it, then! Shape
it! I would not have things cool.   215

Exeunt.

Scene III. [A room in the Garter Inn.]

Enter Host and Bardolph.

Bar. Sir, the Germans desire to have three of your
horses. The Duke himself will be tomorrow at Court,
and they are going to meet him.

Host. What duke should that be comes so secretly?
I hear not of him in the Court. Let me speak with the   5
gentlemen. They speak English?

Bar. Ay, sir. I'll call them to you.

Host. They shall have my horses; but I'll make them

11. **sauce them:** charge them plenty.

||||||||||||||||||||||||||||||||||||||||||||||||||||||

IV.iv. Ford and Page, told of the tricks their wives have played on Falstaff, feel that more sport can be made of him. The women propose that they make an appointment to meet Falstaff, dressed as the mythical Herne the Hunter, in Windsor Forest. Anne Page and a company of others will pretend to be fairies and pinch him unmercifully. Page privately plans to arrange for Slender to elope with Anne Page on this occasion, while Mrs. Page sets out to inform Dr. Caius that this will be his chance to steal her daughter.

||||||||||||||||||||||||||||||||||||||

1. **the best discretions of a oman:** the most discreet women.

pay. I'll sauce them: they have had my house a week
at command. I have turned away my other guests.   10
They must come off. I'll sauce them. Come.

Exeunt.

Scene IV. [A room in Ford's house.]

*Enter Page, Ford, Mistress Page, Mistress Ford, and
Sir Hugh Evans.*

Evans. 'Tis one of the best discretions of a oman as
ever I did look upon.

Page. And did he send you both these letters at an
instant?

Mrs. Page. Within a quarter of an hour.   5

Ford. Pardon me, wife. Henceforth do what thou
  wilt.
I rather will suspect the sun with cold
Than thee with wantonness. Now doth thy honor
  stand,   10
In him that was of late an heretic,
As firm as faith.

Page.   'Tis well, 'tis well: no more!
Be not as extreme in submission
As in offense.   15
But let our plot go forward. Let our wives
Yet once again, to make us public sport,
Appoint a meeting with this old fat fellow,

38. **takes:** bewitches.
42. **eld:** old folk.
45. **want:** lack.

NOBLE MAN

A German nobleman.
From John Speed, *A Prospect of the Most Famous Parts
of the World* (1631).

Where we may take him and disgrace him for it.

Ford. There is no better way than that they spoke   20
of.

Page. How? To send him word they'll meet him in
the park at midnight? Fie, fie! he'll never come.

Evans. You say he has been thrown in the rivers and
has been grievously peaten as an old oman. Methinks   25
there should be terrors in him that he should not
come. Methinks his flesh is punished, he shall have no
desires.

Page. So think I too.

Mrs. Ford. Devise but how you'll use him when he   30
    comes,
And let us two devise to bring him thither.

Mrs. Page. There is an old tale goes that Herne the
    Hunter,
Sometime a keeper here in Windsor forest,   35
Doth all the wintertime, at still midnight,
Walk round about an oak, with great ragg'd horns;
And there he blasts the tree, and takes the cattle,
And makes milch kine yield blood, and shakes a chain
In a most hideous and dreadful manner.   40
You have heard of such a spirit; and well you know
The superstitious idle-headed eld
Received, and did deliver to our age,
This tale of Herne the Hunter for a truth.

Page. Why, yet there want not many that do fear   45
In deep of night to walk by this Herne's oak.
But what of this?

58. **urchins, ouphs:** imps.
63. **diffused:** disordered.

Mrs. Ford.   Marry, this is our device,
That Falstaff at that oak shall meet with us,
Disguised like Herne with huge horns on his head.   50
Page. Well, let it not be doubted but he'll come:
And in this shape when you have brought him thither,
What shall be done with him? What is your plot?
Mrs. Page. That likewise have we thought upon,
      and thus: 55
Nan Page my daughter, and my little son,
And three or four more of their growth we'll dress
Like urchins, ouphs, and fairies, green and white,
With rounds of waxen tapers on their heads,
And rattles in their hands. Upon a sudden,   60
As Falstaff, she, and I are newly met,
Let them from forth a sawpit rush at once
With some diffused song. Upon their sight,
We two in great amazedness will fly:
Then let them all encircle him about,   65
And, fairy-like, to pinch the unclean knight,
And ask him why, that hour of fairy revel,
In their so sacred paths he dares to tread
In shape profane.
Mrs. Ford.   And till he tell the truth,   70
Let the supposed fairies pinch him sound,
And burn him with their tapers.
Mrs. Page.   The truth being known,
We'll all present ourselves, dis-horn the spirit,
And mock him home to Windsor.   75
Ford.   The children must
Be practiced well to this, or they'll ne'er do't.

82. **vizards:** masks.
93. **tricking:** apparel.
100. **well landed:** rich in land.
101. **affects:** prefers.

Evans. I will teach the children their behaviors; and I will be like a jackanapes also, to burn the knight with my taber.   80

Ford. That will be excellent. I'll go buy them vizards.

Mrs. Page. My Nan shall be the queen of all the
fairies,
Finely attired in a robe of white.   85

Page. That silk will I go buy. [*Aside*] And in that
time
Shall Master Slender steal my Nan away
And marry her at Eton. Go send to Falstaff straight.

Ford. Nay, I'll to him again in name of Brook.   90
He'll tell me all his purpose. Sure, he'll come.

Mrs. Page. Fear not you that. Go get us properties
And tricking for our fairies.

Evans. Let us about it: it is admirable pleasures and
fery honest knaveries.   95

                    [*Exeunt Page, Ford, and Evans.*]
Mrs. Page. Go, Mistress Ford,
Send quickly to Sir John, to know his mind.
                    [*Exit Mrs. Ford.*]
I'll to the doctor: he hath my good will,
And none but he, to marry with Nan Page.
That Slender, though well landed, is an idiot;   100
And he my husband best of all affects.
The doctor is well moneyed, and his friends
Potent at court: he, none but he, shall have her,
Though twenty thousand worthier come to crave her.
                    [*Exit.*]

IV.v. Simple seeks the old woman of Brainford at Falstaff's room to learn whether Slender shall win Anne Page. Falstaff gives the fool an ambiguous answer which nevertheless satisfies him. Bardolph reports to the host that the Germans have made off with his horses, and Evans and Caius take delight in assuring him that three Germans have cheated innkeepers in several other towns and that the German duke does not exist. Falstaff is musing on the manner in which he himself has been cheated when Quickly delivers a letter from Mrs. Ford and Mrs. Page.

<hr>

6. **truckle bed:** a small, low bed that was stored under the **standing bed** and usually occupied by a child or a servant.

8. **anthropophaginian:** cannibal.

16. **Ephesian:** boon companion; slang for one who enjoys reveling.

Scene V. [A room in the Garter Inn.]

Enter Host and Simple.

Host. What wouldst thou have, boor? what, thick-
skin? Speak, breathe, discuss: brief, short, quick, snap!

Sim. Marry, sir, I come to speak with Sir John Falstaff from Master Slender.

Host. There's his chamber, his house, his castle, his   5
standing bed and truckle bed; 'tis painted about with
the story of the Prodigal, fresh and new. Go knock
and call. He'll speak like an anthropophaginian unto
thee. Knock, I say.

Sim. There's an old woman, a fat woman, gone up   10
into his chamber. I'll be so bold as stay, sir, till she
come down: I come to speak with her, indeed.

Host. Ha! a fat woman! The knight may be robbed:
I'll call. Bully knight! Bully Sir John! Speak from thy
lungs military. Art thou there? It is thine host, thine   15
Ephesian, calls.

Fal. [*Above*] How now, mine host!

Host. Here's a Bohemian-Tartar tarries the coming
down of thy fat woman. Let her descend, bully, let
her descend. My chambers are honorable. Fie! Pri-   20
vacy! fie!

26. **mussel shell:** probably signifying a useless object.

30. **beguiled:** cheated.

[*Enter Falstaff.*]

Fal. There was, mine host, an old fat woman even now with me; but she's gone.

Sim. Pray you, sir, was't not the wise woman of Brainford?   25

Fal. Ay, marry, was it, mussel shell. What would you with her?

Sim. My master, sir, my master Slender, sent to her, seeing her go through the streets, to know, sir, whether one Nym, sir, that beguiled him of a chain,   30 had the chain or no.

Fal. I spake with the old woman about it.

Sim. And what says she, I pray, sir?

Fal. Marry, she says that the very same man that beguiled Master Slender of his chain cozened him of   35 it.

Sim. I would I could have spoken with the woman herself: I had other things to have spoken with her, too, from him.

Fal. What are they? Let us know.   40

Host. Ay, come, quick!

Sim. I may not conceal them, sir.

Host. Conceal them, or thou diest.

Sim. Why, sir, they were nothing but about Mistress Anne Page: to know if it were my master's fortune to   45 have her or no.

Fal. 'Tis, 'tis his fortune.

55. **clerkly:** i.e., a scholar.

58–9. **more wit than ever I learned before in my life. And I paid nothing for it neither:** an allusion to the proverb "Wit (wisdom) is never good till it be bought."

67–8. **three Doctor Faustuses:** in Christopher Marlowe's *Doctor Faustus* a man is cheated by Faustus and Mephistophilis by means of a phantom horse that disappears when ridden into the water.

The Windsor area of Berkshire.
From John Speed, *A Prospect of the Most Famous Parts of the World* (1631).

Sim. What, sir?

Fal. To have her, or no. Go, say the woman told me
so.   50

Sim. May I be bold to say so, sir?

Fal. Ay, sir, like who more bold?

Sim. I thank your Worship. I shall make my master
glad with these tidings.   [*Exit.*]

Host. Thou art clerkly, thou art clerkly, Sir John.   55
Was there a wise woman with thee?

Fal. Ay, that there was, mine host; one that hath
taught me more wit than ever I learned before in my
life. And I paid nothing for it neither, but was paid for
my learning.   60

[*Enter Bardolph.*]

Bar. Out, alas, sir! cozenage, mere cozenage!

Host. Where be my horses? Speak well of them,
varletto.

Bar. Run away with the cozeners: for so soon as I
came beyond Eton they threw me off, from behind   65
one of them, in a slough of mire, and set spurs and
away, like three German devils, three Doctor
Faustuses.

Host. They are gone but to meet the Duke, villain.
Do not say they be fled: Germans are honest men.   70

[*Enter Sir Hugh Evans.*]

Evans. Where is mine host?

73. **your entertainments:** i.e., whom you welcome to the inn.

75. **cousin-germans:** literally, near relatives, with a pun on "cozening Germans."

95. **liquor:** oil.

Host. What is the matter, sir?

Evans. Have a care of your entertainments. There
is a friend of mine come to town, tells me there is
three cousin-germans that has cozened all the hosts   75
of Readins, of Maidenhead, of Colebrook, of horses
and money. I tell you for good will, look you. You are
wise, and full of gibes and vloutingstocks, and 'tis not
convenient you should be cozened. Fare you well.
                                                    [*Exit.*]

[*Enter Doctor Caius.*]

Caius. Vere is mine host de Jarteer?   80

Host. Here, Master Doctor, in perplexity and
doubtful dilemma.

Caius. I cannot tell vat is dat: but it is tell-a me dat
you make grand preparation for a Duke de Jamany.
By my trot, dere is no duke that the Court is know to   85
come. I tell you for good will. Adieu.   [*Exit.*]

Host. Hue and cry, villain, go! Assist me, knight. I
am undone! Fly, run, hue and cry, villain! I am undone!   [*Exeunt Host and Bardolph.*]

Fal. I would all the world might be cozened; for I   90
have been cozened and beaten too. If it should come
to the ear of the Court how I have been transformed,
and how my transformation hath been washed and
cudgeled, they would melt me out of my fat drop by
drop and liquor fishermen's boots with me. I warrant   95
they would whip me with their fine wits till I were as

98. forswore: perjured; **primero:** a card game.

crestfallen as a dried pear. I never prospered since
I forswore myself at primero. Well, if my wind were
but long enough to say my prayers, I would repent.

[*Enter Mistress Quickly.*]

Now, whence come you?   100

Quick. From the two parties, forsooth.

Fal. The Devil take one party and his dam the
other! and so they shall be both bestowed. I have suffered more for their sakes, more than the villainous
inconstancy of man's disposition is able to bear.   105

Quick. And have not they suffered? Yes, I warrant;
speciously one of them. Mistress Ford, good heart, is
beaten black and blue, that you cannot see a white
spot about her.

Fal. What tellst thou me of black and blue? I was 110
beaten myself into all the colors of the rainbow; and I
was like to be apprehended for the witch of Brainford.
But that my admirable dexterity of wit, my counter-
feiting the action of an old woman, delivered me, the
knave constable had set me i' the stocks, i' the com- 115
mon stocks, for a witch.

Quick. Sir, let me speak with you in your chamber.
You shall hear how things go; and, I warrant, to your
content. Here is a letter will say somewhat. Good
hearts, what ado here is to bring you together! Sure, 120
one of you does not serve Heaven well, that you are
so crossed.

IV.vi. Fenton enlists the host's aid in arranging an elopement with Anne Page. Her father has planned that she be dressed in white and Slender will seek her in that dress; her mother has arranged that she wear green ribbons so that Dr. Caius may recognize her. Fenton has her promise to elude the other two and go with him, and he asks the host to secure the services of the vicar to marry them that night.

▄▄▄▄▄▄▄▄▄▄▄▄▄▄▄▄▄▄▄▄▄▄▄▄▄

14. **larded:** mingled.
18. **at large:** in full.
19. **just:** exactly.
20. **present:** represent.

Fal. Come up into my chamber.

Exeunt.

Scene VI. [Another room in the Garter Inn.]

Enter Fenton and Host.

Host. Master Fenton, talk not to me; my mind is
heavy: I will give over all.

Fen. Yet hear me speak. Assist me in my purpose,
And, as I am a gentleman, I'll give thee
A hundred pound in gold more than your loss.   5

Host. I will hear you, Master Fenton; and I will at
the least keep your counsel.

Fen. From time to time I have acquainted you
With the dear love I bear to fair Anne Page;
Who mutually hath answered my affection,   10
So far forth as herself might be her chooser,
Even to my wish. I have a letter from her
Of such contents as you will wonder at;
The mirth whereof so larded with my matter
That neither singly can be manifested   15
Without the show of both; wherein fat Falstaff
Hath a great scene. The image of the jest
I'll show you here at large. Hark, good mine host.
Tonight at Herne's oak, just 'twixt twelve and one,
Must my sweet Nan present the Fairy Queen—   20
The purpose why is here [*Shows Host a letter*]—in
    which disguise,

23. **While other jests are something rank on foot:** i.e., while the other conspirators are busy with their tricks.

31. **tasking of:** occupying.

42. **quaint:** cleverly or elegantly.

43. **ribands:** ribbons.

44. **vantage:** opportunity.

50. **here it rests:** here is the conclusion.

While other jests are something rank on foot,
Her father hath commanded her to slip
Away with Slender and with him at Eton   25
Immediately to marry. She hath consented.
Now, sir,
Her mother, even strong against that match
And firm for Doctor Caius, hath appointed
That he shall likewise shuffle her away,   30
While other sports are tasking of their minds,
And at the deanery, where a priest attends,
Straight marry her. To this her mother's plot
She seemingly obedient likewise hath
Made promise to the doctor. Now, thus it rests: 35
Her father means she shall be all in white;
And in that habit, when Slender sees his time
To take her by the hand and bid her go,
She shall go with him. Her mother hath intended,
The better to denote her to the doctor—   40
For they must all be masked and vizarded—
That quaint in green she shall be loose enrobed,
With ribands pendent, flaring 'bout her head;
And when the doctor spies his vantage ripe,
To pinch her by the hand, and, on that token,   45
The maid hath given consent to go with him.

   Host. Which means she to deceive, father or
    mother?

   Fen. Both, my good host, to go along with me.
And here it rests: that you'll procure the vicar   50
To stay for me at church 'twixt twelve and one,
And, in the lawful name of marrying,

53. **united ceremony:** i.e., a ceremony of union; marriage.

54. **husband:** take good care of.

To give our hearts united ceremony.

Host. Well, husband your device: I'll to the vicar.
Bring you the maid, you shall not lack a priest.   55

Fen. So shall I evermore be bound to thee.
Besides, I'll make a present recompense.

Exeunt.

THE
MERRY WIVES
OF
WINDSOR

ACT V

V.i. Falstaff has agreed to meet the two women, and Quickly undertakes to supply the furnishings for his garb as Herne the Hunter. Ford as Brook comes to learn of Falstaff's progress, and the old rogue boasts that he will be revenged on Ford that very night for the beating he has suffered.

▓▓▓▓▓▓▓▓▓▓▓▓▓▓▓▓▓▓▓

1. **hold:** keep my promise to come.
3. **divinity:** divination.
8. **mince:** be on your way (with reference to Quickly's characteristic gait).

ACT V

Scene I. [A room in the Garter Inn.]

Enter Falstaff and Mistress Quickly.

Fal. Prithee, no more prattling: go! I'll hold. This is the third time. I hope good luck lies in odd numbers. Away! go! They say there is divinity in odd numbers, either in nativity, chance, or death. Away!

Quick. I'll provide you a chain, and I'll do what I   5 can to get you a pair of horns.

Fal. Away, I say! time wears. Hold up your head and mince.   *[Exit Mrs. Quickly.]*

[Enter Ford (Brook).]

How now, Master Brook! Master Brook, the matter will be known tonight, or never. Be you in the park   10 about midnight, at Herne's oak, and you shall see wonders.

Ford. Went you not to her yesterday, sir, as you told me you had appointed?

Fal. I went to her, Master Brook, as you see, like a   15 poor old man; but I came from her, Master Brook, like a poor old woman. That same knave Ford, her

22–3. **life is a shuttle:** a proverbial idea deriving from Job 7:6.

▪▪▪

V.ii. Page, Slender, and Shallow await the appearance of the "fairies."

▪▪▪▪▪▪▪▪▪▪▪▪▪▪▪▪▪▪▪▪▪▪▪▪▪▪▪▪

1. **couch:** hide.
6. **"mum"** . . . **"budget":** "mumbudget" was a catchword for "silence." **Mum** suggests keeping silent and **budget** is a term for a wallet or pouch; therefore, "keep a closed pouch (mouth)."

husband, hath the finest mad devil of jealousy in him,
Master Brook, that ever governed frenzy. I will tell
you. He beat me grievously, in the shape of a woman;   20
for in the shape of man, Master Brook, I fear not
Goliath with a weaver's beam, because I know also life
is a shuttle. I am in haste. Go along with me: I'll tell
you all, Master Brook. Since I plucked geese, played
truant, and whipped top, I knew not what 'twas to be   25
beaten till lately. Follow me: I'll tell you strange
things of this knave Ford, on whom tonight I will be
revenged, and I will deliver his wife into your hand.
Follow. Strange things in hand, Master Brook! Follow!
                                        Exeunt.

Scene II. [Windsor Park.]

Enter Page, Shallow, and Slender.

Page. Come, come! we'll couch i' the castle ditch
till we see the light of our fairies. Remember, son
Slender, my daughter.

Slen. Ay, forsooth. I have spoke with her, and we
have a nayword how to know one another: I come   5
to her in white, and cry, "mum"; she cries "budget";
and by that we know one another.

Shal. That's good too: but what needs either your
"mum" or her "budget"? The white will decipher her
well enough. It hath struck ten o'clock.   10

V.iii. Mrs. Page informs Dr. Caius that her daughter will be in green. She and Mrs. Ford then set themselves to await the unfolding of their little plot against Falstaff.

Page. The night is dark; light and spirits will become it well. Heaven prosper our sport! No man means evil but the Devil, and we shall know him by his horns. Let's away. Follow me.

Exeunt.

Scene III. [A street leading to the park.]

Enter Mistress Page, Mistress Ford, and Doctor Caius.

Mrs. Page. Master Doctor, my daughter is in green: when you see your time, take her by the hand, away with her to the deanery, and dispatch it quickly. Go before into the park; we two must go together.

Caius. I know vat I have to do. Adieu.   5

Mrs. Page. Fare you well, sir [*Exit Caius.*] My husband will not rejoice so much at the abuse of Falstaff as he will chafe at the doctor's marrying my daughter; but 'tis no matter: better a little chiding than a great deal of heartbreak.   10

Mrs. Ford. Where is Nan now and her troop of fairies, and the Welsh devil Hugh?

Mrs. Page. They are all couched in a pit hard by Herne's oak, with obscured lights, which, at the very instant of Falstaff's and our meeting, they will at once   15 display to the night.

Mrs. Ford. That cannot choose but amaze him.

Mrs. Page. If he be not amazed, he will be mocked. If he be amazed, he will every way be mocked.

V.iv. Evans, disguised as a satyr, herds the disguised fairies to their places in the forest.

━━━━━━━━━━━━━━━━━━━━━━━━━━━━━━━━

V.v. Falstaff, wearing a buck's head, seeks his mistresses at the appointed place. As he is embracing them, horns announce the arrival of the fairy crew. Anne as the fairy queen orders the company to pinch and torment Falstaff. As they burn him with tapers, she sings a song reproaching him for his lust. Dr. Caius in the meantime steals away with a fairy in green and Slender with another in white, while Fenton goes off with the real Anne Page. Page and Ford remain with their wives and Falstaff, to whom they reveal that he has again been duped. Ford also informs Falstaff that he was the Master Brook who gave him twenty pounds to seduce Mrs. Ford and that he expects repayment. The Pages each are congratulating themselves that Anne is safely married to the man of their own choice when Slender appears and complains that he has found himself about to be married to a boy, and Caius relates the same experience. Fenton and Anne then enter and reveal that they have been married. The parents accept their defeat philosophically, and Mrs. Page invites the company to the Page home to have a laugh over the complicated intrigues that are finally resolved.

Mrs. Ford. We'll betray him finely.   20

Mrs. Page. Against such lewdsters and their lechery
Those that betray them do no treachery.

Mrs. Ford. The hour draws on. To the oak, to the
oak!

Exeunt.

Scene IV. [Windsor Park.]

*Enter [Sir Hugh] Evans [disguised as a satyr, and
others as] fairies.*

Evans. Trib, trib, fairies. Come, and remember your
parts. Be pold, I pray you. Follow me into the pit;
and when I give the watch-ords, do as I pid you.
Come, come; trib, trib.

Exeunt.

Scene V. [Another part of the park.]

*Enter Falstaff [disguised as Herne, with a buck's head
upon him].*

Fal. The Windsor bell hath struck twelve; the minute draws on. Now, the hot-blooded gods assist me!
Remember, Jove, thou wast a bull for thy Europa:
love set on thy horns. O powerful love! that in some

18. **scut:** tail.

19. **potatoes:** considered an aphrodisiac.

20. **kissing-comfits:** perfumed confections (to sweeten the breath); **eryngoes:** candied sea-holly root, another supposed aphrodisiac.

24. **bribed:** poached.

25–6. **my shoulders for the fellow of this walk:** the shoulder was the share given to the game-keeper (**fellow of this walk**) when a deer was killed.

27. **a woodman:** a skilled forester and huntsman.

Jove in bull's shape and Europa.
From Gabrieli Simeoni, *La vita et Metamorfoseo d'Ovidio* (1559).

respects makes a beast a man, in some other, a man a   5
beast. You were also, Jupiter, a swan for the love of
Leda. O omnipotent love! how near the god drew to
the complexion of a goose! A fault done first in the
form of a beast. O Jove, a beastly fault! And then another fault in the semblance of a fowl: think on't,   10
Jove; a foul fault! When gods have hot backs, what
shall poor men do? For me, I am here a Windsor stag,
and the fattest, I think, i' the forest. Send me a cool
rut time, Jove, or who can blame me to piss my tal-
low? Who comes here? My doe?   15

[*Enter Mistress Ford and Mistress Page.*]

Mrs. Ford. Sir John! art thou there, my deer? my
male deer?
Fal. My doe with the black scut! Let the sky rain
potatoes; let it thunder to the tune of "Greensleeves,"
hail kissing-comfits, and snow eryngoes. Let there   20
come a tempest of provocation. I will shelter me here.
[*Embracing her.*]
Mrs. Ford. Mistress Page is come with me, sweetheart.
Fal. Divide me like a bribed buck, each a haunch:
I will keep my sides to myself, my shoulders for the   25
fellow of this walk, and my horns I bequeath your
husbands. Am I a woodman, ha? Speak I like Herne
the Hunter? Why, now is Cupid a child of conscience:
he makes restitution. As I am a true spirit, welcome!
[*Noise of horns within.*]

40. **quality:** profession.

41. **make the fairy oyes:** call the fairy company to order.

49. **wink:** close my eyes. It was considered dangerous to observe fairy rites.

Mrs. Page. Alas, what noise?   30
Mrs. Ford. Heaven forgive our sins!
Fal. What should this be?
Mrs. Ford. ⎫
Mrs. Page. ⎭ Away, away!   [*They run off.*]
Fal. I think the Devil will not have me damned,
Lest the oil that's in me should set hell on fire: 35
He would never else cross me thus.

[*Enter Sir Hugh Evans, disguised; Pistol, as Hobgoblin; Anne Page, as Fairy Queen, and others as Fairies,
                    with tapers.*]

Anne. Fairies, black, gray, green, and white,
You moonshine revelers and shades of night,
You orphan heirs of fixed destiny,
Attend your office and your quality.   40
Crier Hobgoblin, make the fairy oyes.
    Pis. Elves, list your names. Silence, you airy toys.
Cricket, to Windsor chimneys shalt thou leap.
Where fires thou findst unraked and hearths unswept,
There pinch the maids as blue as bilberry: 45
Our radiant Queen hates sluts and sluttery.
    Fal. They are fairies: he that speaks to them shall
        die.
I'll wink and couch: no man their works must eye.
                            [*Lies down upon his face.*]
    Evans. Where's Bede? Go you, and where you find   50
        a maid
That, ere she sleep, has thrice her prayers said,

53. **fantasy:** fancy.

54. **Sleep she:** may she sleep.

55. **as:** who.

64. **chairs of order:** stalls belonging to the Knights of the Order of the Garter.

66. **installment:** stall; seat; **sev'ral:** individual.

67. **blazon:** heraldic shield or coat of arms.

69. **the Garter's compass:** the circle in the insignia of the Garter.

70. **expressure:** impression; depiction.

72. **Honi soit qui mal y pense:** the Garter motto: "Evil to him who evil thinks."

76. **charactery:** writing.

78. **dance of custom:** customary dance.

Garter Badge.

The badge of the Garter Herald.
From Elias Ashmole, *The Institution, Laws, and Ceremonies of the Most Noble Order of the Garter* (1672).

Raise up the organs of her fantasy,
Sleep she as sound as careless infancy;
But those as sleep and think not on their sins,   55
Pinch them, arms, legs, backs, shoulders, sides, and
    shins.
  Anne. About, about;
Search Windsor Castle, elves, within and out.
Strew good luck, ouphs, on every sacred room,   60
That it may stand till the perpetual doom
In state as wholesome as in state 'tis fit,
Worthy the owner, and the owner it.
The several chairs of order look you scour
With juice of balm and every precious flower.   65
Each fair installment, coat, and sev'ral crest,
With loyal blazon, evermore be blest!
And nightly, meadow fairies, look you sing,
Like to the Garter's compass, in a ring.
The expressure that it bears, green let it be,   70
More fertile-fresh than all the field to see;
And *Honi soit qui mal y pense* write
In em'rald tufts, flow'rs purple, blue, and white;
Like sapphire, pearl, and rich embroidery,
Buckled below fair knighthood's bending knee.   75
Fairies use flow'rs for their charactery.
Away, disperse! But till 'tis one o'clock,
Our dance of custom round about the oak
Of Herne the Hunter let us not forget.
  Evans. Pray you, lock hand in hand; yourselves in   80
    order set;
And twenty glowworms shall our lanterns be,

83. **measure:** dance.

84. **middle-earth:** an old term, the earth being conceived as midway between heaven and hell.

87. **o'erlooked:** enchanted.

89. **touch me:** touch for me.

98. **still:** always.

100. **luxury:** synonymous with **lust.**

105. **mutually:** each simultaneously.

To guide our measure round about the tree.
But, stay! I smell a man of middle-earth.

   Fal. Heavens defend me from that Welsh fairy,   85
Lest he transform me to a piece of cheese!

   Pis. Vile worm, thou wast o'erlooked even in thy
    birth.

   Anne. With trial fire touch me his finger end:
If he be chaste, the flame will back descend   90
And turn him to no pain; but if he start,
It is the flesh of a corrupted heart.

   Pis. A trial, come.

   Evans.   Come, will this wood take fire?

           [*They burn him with their tapers.*]

   Fal. Oh, Oh, Oh!   95

   Anne. Corrupt, corrupt, and tainted in desire!
About him, fairies: sing a scornful rhyme,
And, as you trip, still pinch him to your time.

The Song.

   Fie on sinful fantasy!
   Fie on lust and luxury!   100
   Lust is but a bloody fire,
   Kindled with unchaste desire,
   Fed in heart, whose flames aspire,
    As thoughts do blow them, higher and higher.
   Pinch him, fairies, mutually;   105
   Pinch him for his villainy;
Pinch him, and burn him, and turn him about,
Till candles and starlight and moonshine be out.

109. **watched:** detected.

112–13. **hold up the jest no higher:** continue the jest no longer.

115. **yokes:** horns (because their curving shape resembled the yokes used on oxen).

[*During this song they pinch Falstaff. Doctor Caius comes one way and steals away a fairy in green; Slender another way and takes off a fairy in white; and Fenton comes and steals away Anne Page. A noise of hunting is heard within. All the fairies run away. Falstaff pulls off his buck's head and rises.*]

[*Enter Page, Ford, Mistress Page and Mistress Ford.*]

Page. Nay, do not fly. I think we have watched you   110
    now.
Will none but Herne the Hunter serve your turn?
    Mrs. Page. I pray you, come, hold up the jest no
        higher.
Now, good Sir John, how like you Windsor wives?
See you these, husband? Do not these fair yokes   115
Become the forest better than the town?
    Ford. Now, sir, who's a cuckold now? Master Brook,
Falstaff's a knave, a cuckoldly knave: here are his
horns, Master Brook. And, Master Brook, he hath
enjoyed nothing of Ford's but his buck basket, his   120
cudgel, and twenty pounds of money, which must be
paid to Master Brook: his horses are arrested for it,
Master Brook.
    Mrs. Ford. Sir John, we have had ill luck: we could
never meet. I will never take you for my love again;   125
but I will always count you my deer.
    Fal. I do begin to perceive that I am made an ass.
    Ford. Ay, and an ox too: both the proofs are extant.
    Fal. And these are not fairies? I was three or four

131. **surprise:** capture.

132. **grossness:** obviousness; **foppery:** deception.

133. **teeth:** i.e., face.

145. **o'erreaching:** outsmarting.

147. **coxcomb:** fool's crested cap; **frieze:** coarse woolen fabric (often of Welsh origin).

times in the thought they were not fairies: and yet 130
the guiltiness of my mind, the sudden surprise of my
powers, drove the grossness of the foppery into a received belief, in despite of the teeth of all rhyme and
reason, that they were fairies. See now how wit may
be made a Jack-a-Lent, when 'tis upon ill employ- 135
ment!

Evans. Sir John Falstaff, serve Got and leave your
desires, and fairies will not pinse you.

Ford. Well said, fairy Hugh.

Evans. And leave you your jealousies too, I pray 140
you.

Ford. I will never mistrust my wife again, till thou
art able to woo her in good English.

Fal. Have I laid my brain in the sun and dried it,
that it wants matter to prevent so gross o'erreaching 145
as this? Am I ridden with a Welsh goat too? Shall I
have a coxcomb of frieze? 'Tis time I were choked
with a piece of toasted cheese.

Evans. Seese is not good to give putter: your belly
is all putter.   150

Fal. "Seese" and "putter"? Have I lived to stand at
the taunt of one that makes fritters of English? This
is enough to be the decay of lust and late walking
through the realm.

Mrs. Page. Why, Sir John, do you think, though we 155
would have thrust virtue out of our hearts by the head
and shoulders, and have given ourselves without
scruple to hell, that ever the Devil could have made
you our delight?

160. **hodge pudding:** pudding made of hog's entrails; **bag of flax:** i.e., shapeless lump.

162–63. **of intolerable entrails:** monstrously fat.

168. **metheglins:** Welsh mead.

169. **starings:** impudent bluster.

170. **start:** advantage.

172. **is a plummet o'er me:** is deeper than I am.

183. **Doctors doubt that:** proverbial.

Ford. What, a hodge pudding? A bag of flax?   160
Mrs. Page. A puffed man?
Page. Old, cold, withered, and of intolerable entrails?
Ford. And one that is as slanderous as Satan?
Page. And as poor as Job?   165
Ford. And as wicked as his wife?
Evans. And given to fornications, and to taverns, and sack, and wine, and metheglins, and to drinkings, and swearings, and starings, pribbles and prabbles?
Fal. Well, I am your theme: you have the start of   170
me. I am dejected. I am not able to answer the Welsh flannel. Ignorance itself is a plummet o'er me. Use me as you will.
Ford. Marry, sir, we'll bring you to Windsor, to one Master Brook, that you have cozened of money, to   175
whom you should have been a pander. Over and above that you have suffered, I think to repay that money will be a biting affliction.
Page. Yet be cheerful, knight: thou shalt eat a posset tonight at my house; where I will desire thee to   180
laugh at my wife, that now laughs at thee. Tell her Master Slender hath married her daughter.
Mrs. Page. [*Aside*] Doctors doubt that: if Anne Page be my daughter, she is, by this, Doctor Caius' wife.   185

[*Enter Slender.*]

Slen. Whoa, ho! ho, father Page!

194. **swinged:** beaten.
196–97. **postmaster:** man who rented post horses.

Page. Son, how now! How now, son! Have you dispatched?

Slen. Dispatched! I'll make the best in Gloucestershire know on't: would I were hanged, la, else!   190

Page. Of what, son?

Slen. I came yonder at Eton to marry Mistress Anne Page, and she's a great lubberly boy. If it had not been i' the church, I would have swinged him, or he should have swinged me. If I did not think it had been   195 Anne Page, would I might never stir! And 'tis a postmaster's boy.

Page. Upon my life, then, you took the wrong.

Slen. What need you tell me that? I think so, when I took a boy for a girl. If I had been married to him,   200 for all he was in woman's apparel, I would not have had him.

Page. Why, this is your own folly. Did not I tell you how you should know my daughter by her garments?

Slen. I went to her in white, and cried "mum," and   205 she cried "budget," as Anne and I had appointed; and yet it was not Anne, but a postmaster's boy.

Mrs. Page. Good George, be not angry: I knew of your purpose, turned my daughter into green; and, indeed, she is now with the doctor at the deanery and   210 there married.

[*Enter Caius.*]

Caius. Vere is Mistress Page? By gar, I am cozened:

228. **amaze:** confuse.

230. **Where there was no proportion held in love:** where mutual love was lacking.

231. **contracted:** betrothed.

232. **sure:** safely married.

236. **evitate:** synonymous with **shun.**

I ha' married *un garçon*, a boy; *un paysan*, by gar, a
boy! It is not Anne Page. By gar, I am cozened!

Mrs. Page. Why, did you take her in green?   215

Caius. Ay, be-gar, and 'tis a boy! Be-gar, I'll raise
all Windsor.   [*Exit.*]

Ford. This is strange. Who hath got the right Anne?

Page. My heart misgives me. Here comes Master
Fenton.   220

[*Enter Fenton and Anne Page.*]

How now, Master Fenton!

Anne. Pardon, good father! Good my mother, pardon!

Page. Now, mistress, how chance you went not with
Master Slender?   225

Mrs. Page. Why went you not with Master Doctor,
maid?

Fen. You do amaze her: hear the truth of it.
You would have married her most shamefully,
Where there was no proportion held in love.   230
The truth is, she and I, long since contracted,
Are now so sure that nothing can dissolve us.
The offense is holy that she hath committed;
And this deceit loses the name of craft,
Of disobedience, or unduteous title,   235
Since therein she doth evitate and shun
A thousand irreligious cursed hours,
Which forced marriage would have brought upon her.

Ford. Stand not amazed: here is no remedy.

240. **In love the Heavens themselves do guide the state:** i.e., marriages are made in Heaven, as the proverb has it.

In love the Heavens themselves do guide the state.   240
Money buys lands, and wives are sold by fate.

Fal. I am glad, though you have ta'en a special
stand to strike at me, that your arrow hath glanced.

Page. Well, what remedy? Fenton, Heaven give
thee joy!   245
What cannot be eschewed must be embraced.

Fal. When night dogs run, all sorts of deer are
chased.

Mrs. Page. Well, I will muse no further. Master
Fenton,   250
Heaven give you many, many merry days!
Good husband, let us every one go home,
And laugh this sport o'er by a country fire,
Sir John and all.

Ford.   Let it be so. Sir John,   255
To Master Brook you yet shall hold your word;
For he tonight shall lie with Mistress Ford.

Exeunt.

KEY TO

Famous Lines

I am almost out at heels.   [*Falstaff*—I. iii. 30]

Here will be an old abusing of God's patience
   and the King's English.   [*Quickly*—I. iv. 4–5]

Why, then the world's mine oyster,
Which I with sword will open.   [*Pistol*—II. ii. 2–3]

This is the short and the long of it.   [*Quickly*—II. ii. 58]

Setting the attraction of my good parts aside,
   I have no other charms.   [*Falstaff*—II. ii. 103–4]

A woman would run through fire and water for
   such a kind heart.   [*Quickly*—III. iv. 110–11]

As good luck would have it.   [*Falstaff*—III. v. 79]

A man of my kidney.   [*Falstaff*—III. v. 108–9]